WHITE BELL HEATHER

WHITE BELL HEATHER

by

ISABEL CAMERON

LUTTERWORTH PRESS
LONDON

PRINTED IN GREAT BRITAIN BY J. AND J. GRAY, EDINBURGH

CONTENTS

CHAPTER I

THE SNOWSTORM

WITH a nerve-shattering shriek, accompanied by a cloud of black smoke from the engine, a clatter of brakes, and a sinister vibration from beneath the carriages, the Highland train came to a standstill.

The passengers—there were two of them—the others having dropped off here and there—thrust their heads out of the carriage windows to ask, 'What's wrong, guard?'

The guard, a short, stocky little man, with a red beard and a humorous cock in his eye, was walking along the footboard busily munching a biscuit and did not reply. It was a large Abernethy biscuit, and everyone who has tackled such a dainty knows how much mastication it takes.

Presently, his mouth being empty, he replied, 'I couldna speak sooner—my mooth was full o' busket—gey dry—I near choked on it. Oh, what's wrang? The snow—that's what's wrang! One flake o' snow's no' so bad, but when the flakes get organized like this . . .' he pointed to the snowy landscape, 'then of coorse the train gets stuck.'

The girl, who was leaning out of the third-class window, looked along the line in the direction of the engine.

'She's up tae the neck,' the guard said, nodding towards the engine, and in reply to the girl's unspoken question. 'I kent when we left Inverness that the drifts were bad, but didna ken they were this bad, and noo it's awa' tae the frost, and the snow's like ice.'

'How long will it be before we get a move on?' The voice came from the first-class passenger, and it was clear he was peeved.

'I couldna say indeed, sir,' said the guard, cheerfully beginning on a second biscuit. 'The relief engine may come from Inverness or it may come from Georgemas Junction— both places are a bittie awa'.'

By this time the engine-driver and the stoker had joined the guard, and the pungent smell of bogie-roll tobacco rose on the frosty air.

The engine-driver, a tall, dark, gloomy-looking man, shook his head when he was asked how long they were to stay marooned on a Highland moor, with great drifts of snow all around them.

The girl shivered and turned up the collar of her tweed coat. 'Are ye cold, mem?' the guard asked sympathetically. After all, she was the only woman-body aboard and something must be done about it.

'I'm cold and I'm hungry,' she said—just like that.

'Losh-be-here.' The guard dived into his pocket and produced a paper bag rather the worse for wear, but in the bottom of it was his last remaining Abernethy biscuit. 'Here ye are, mem—better nor nothing—an' there's a box o' kippered herring yonder in my van. If the warst comes tae the warst, we can roast a couple on the van stove.'

She nodded her thanks, her mouth being too full for speech.

The gloomy engine-driver was confiding to the guard that he had a can of milk and a few fresh eggs for Hector Macphail, the gamekeeper, at Corry Buie. These dainties were needed for Hector, who was ill, and they were to be delivered at Auchinah station, but with the storm there was no hope of reaching the station. 'I would walk to the house,' said the driver, ' but I'm afraid to leave my engine in case the water'll go off the bile.'

The girl—her name was Barbara Murray—had been listening, and now she suggested that if the gamekeeper's house wasn't too far away she'd go with the milk and eggs to the sick man.

The guard demurred. 'The snow's as hard as flint,' he said, 'an' it's awfu' cold, an' the hoose is a good bit off.'

'Pooh, nonsense,' she said, joining them on the footboard. 'Just tell me where the house is, and I'll go. The walk will warm me.'

'It's only a mile an' a bittock,' the engine-driver said.

'It's twa miles onyway,' the guard demurred, 'an' coorse walking.'

He pointed to a distant plume of smoke, which certainly looked a long way off. 'That's the hoose, an' if ye say that Malcolm Maciver the guard sent you—they'll be awfu' kind tae ye; the keeper's in his bed, but Merran is a friendly bit body and kind tae ony one that needs it—no' a bit particular.'

The first-class passenger had been looking and listening. 'I'll come with you, if I may,' he said. 'Please allow me to carry these things —I can put the eggs in my pocket,' which he did.

First-class passengers are beings apart, and are always regarded with a certain amount of suspicion by their less-exalted fellow men and women. Barbara looked at the man's well-cut overcoat, his expensive-looking gloves. Still, there was no time to study social distinctions, and the plight they were in forbade it, so she smiled and said, 'I'll carry the milk-can.' For the time being, they were equals, sharing an equal fate.

Malcolm the guard gave them further directions. 'An' when the relief train comes in, we'll blow the whistle,' he added kindly, 'an' the engine'll *toot and toot* till ye come. Oh, ye'll hear it all right.'

As the two passengers set off on their parlous way the guard said, with a twinkle in his eye to the driver, 'It strikes me they'll wait a gey whilie before they hear the *toot-toot* o' the engine. The snow's that hard they're telling me they have tae tak' a pick-axe tae it.'

Meanwhile Barbara and her companion were making but slow progress. In the hollow places the snow was soft and up to their knees—on the higher ground it was as hard as ice and as slippery, so that more than once they fell.

'Oh, take care of the eggs,' Barbara called in alarm, when her companion rolled down a bank.

He looked ruefully at her as he picked himself up. 'What about my bones?' he asked.

'You haven't broken any?'

'Bones or eggs?'

She laughed—so did he, and put his hand

gingerly into his pocket. 'By some act of God, they're still whole,' he said solemnly.

'And your bones?'

'I'm hoping they have also escaped. I'll know all particulars better by to-morrow.'

The air was icy-cold and like wine—even if they did fall they rose again, and the exercise in the frosty air made their faces tingle, and sent their blood dancing through their veins. They felt as if they were old friends, and took turn about of carrying the precious eggs (one, unfortunately, had got broken, and she proposed they'd eat it—or drink it—what does one do with a raw egg?). It was a shame to throw off the mercies. He said generously, 'You take it, then.'

She made a face. 'A broken raw egg is not a pretty object,' she said. 'I'll just lay it here in the snow—perhaps some deserving bird or beast may get it.'

A herd of hungry-looking deer gazed down at them from a height; they could see the footprints of all sorts of furred and feathered creatures in the snow; an angry cock-grouse told them to 'go back, go back, go back,' and beside a burn they came on a dead stag.

He lay, the beautiful beast, with his head resting on the bank and his eyes closed, pathetic and helpless. He had often escaped death at the hands of the hunter, but death had met him this cruel winter, and it was death from starvation, not from a gun-shot.

The two travellers stood looking down at the dead deer. 'Poor, pretty beast,' Barbara said. 'Even in death he looks like a king.'

His stomach was quite empty—when he had come to the burn for a drink, the water was frozen, and so he had laid him down and died.

There is something unspeakably touching in the patient silence with which an animal accepts his fate, and the travellers walked on musing over what they had seen.

'That mile and a bittock seem to be endless,' Barbara said at last. 'I've lost sight of the smoke. Have you?'

He admitted that he had. They were surrounded by snow, white and dazzling, and except for the footprints of birds and beasts it was quite trackless.

They stumbled on in silence; the short winter day was drawing to a close; already the sun was sending a red, frosty glow over the western sky.

'Doesn't that look like a little house?' Barbara asked, pointing to something which looked like an unusually large snowdrift.

When they came nearer, they found it was a roughly built wooden bothy, used by the roadmen when they were repairing the roads: it had a little lean-to at the back, evidently used for storing fuel.

The door was locked, but the young man put his shoulder to it, and burst it open. It was a shelter of sorts, but anything drearier on a cold winter evening it would be hard to imagine.

The small window was covered with snow, there were a couple of chairs, a rough-looking table, and an upturned box which called itself a dresser, and had upon it a few coarse cups and bowls, and, beneath, a rusty-looking kettle, a frying-pan, and an enamel basin. The bothy was dark, and over everything hung the depressing smell of a burnt-out peat fire. They explored the place, and discovered a paraffin lamp which had still some oil in it, and in the lean-to a heap of peats.

'There's a moon,' Barbara said hopefully. 'Perhaps if we waited here for a little till the moon rose we could reach the gamekeeper's house. Have you matches?'

He had—he had been proposing to himself to use one to light his pipe and wondering could he offer her a cigarette.

'The lamp,' she said briefly, and collapsed on a chair.

When the lamp was lighted, he saw that her face had gone pale, and she was biting her underlip.

'Is—is—anything wrong?'

She tried to laugh. 'My shoes were new and I've blistered my heel—my right heel—and the pain is . . .' She bit her lip again.

He looked about him in a helpless fashion. What does one do with a blistered heel?—Bathe it in hot water? Aye, but where was the fire or the water? He hurled (silent) maledictions at his friend Adam Cormack who had chosen to be married in the month of December and in such an out-of-the-world place as Thorwick, and why on earth had he—Andrew Blackwood—ever agreed to act as his best man? But for his own good nature he had never been in this plight, and what was he to do now? He frowned, and looked severely at the girl.

She seemed to divine his thoughts. 'I really could not help it,' she said. 'It's dark now—I think if you went out and scanned the horizon you might see the light in the gamekeeper's house. The moor is so flat it should be easily seen.'

'And leave you?'

'I'll be all right,' she said bravely. She had grey eyes, fearless and frank - looking, there was a hint of banter in them now, her chin was firm, and her mouth shared the mockery in her eyes, but it was a nice mouth too, and her voice, soft and Highland, was full of pretty notes that somehow made quite ordinary words seem memorable. She was tall and slim and supple. Already he had admired the way she walked— it reminded him of a deer stepping daintily over the heather. And all the while her heel had been hurting her . . . well, she was brave!

'I heard you tell the guard you were hungry. Would you like another biscuit?'

'I would—I'm ready to cry with hunger,' she confessed.

'Are you sure it isn't with pain?'

'Quite sure. Do you, like Malcolm the guard, carry Abernethy biscuits, too?'

He said, 'Yes,' and examined the milk-pail. The milk was solid. 'There are peats,' she hinted, for she was desperately cold, 'and there may be sticks in the back place—we could take a little paraffin out of the lamp to start the fire.'

He handed her a biscuit; it was soft, all the crispness had gone out of it, but she ate it with relish, while he went on a tour of exploration.

He came back with a bag of damp sugar and a wooden box which had once held margarine.

'Cheers!' she cried, and directed him, from the chair where she sat, how to build a peat fire—she even hopped on one leg in order to show how the peats must be broken into small pieces if you wished a speedy fire. Then she sprinkled a generous handful of sugar over everything, and lit a match.

'I've a good mind to smash a chair,' he said recklessly. The bothy was full of smoke, which made their eyes smart and filled their throats with dust. He reproached her with having wasted sugar, and all in vain.

'Already you've thrown away a good egg,' he reminded her, 'and now sugar, by the handful.'

'But look,' she said triumphantly, 'the fire is taking.' A little tongue of flame came licking round the brown sods—it grew stronger—was joined by others and then by others. 'I don't think we'll need to sacrifice the chair after all,' she said thankfully, and drew nearer the hearth.

He set the frozen milk-can near the flames and was instantly rebuked for doing so.

'I'd like you to take the milk to the game-keeper's just as it is,' she said. 'I know you are planning to give me some, and although my baser nature says "Yes" my better nature says "No." I'm sure the sick man needs it more than I do.'

'I don't approve of engines being used to run about delivering cans of milk. I'm sure if the ill-paid shareholders knew they'd be indignant.'

His eyes twinkled; he'd rather nice dark eyes, she thought, and his hair matched them, except round his ears, where it was frosted with grey. Though it was obvious he had never built a peat fire before, Barbara admired the deft way his hands, thin, brown and well kept, did the work; they were the hands of a thinker and scholar.

The ruddy glow of the fire by this time transformed the cheerless bothy, and made it almost home-like and cosy. Queer that a fire can work such a miracle! Not only was there warmth—there was a sense of intimacy, of experiences shared, of comradeship.

'If I'd fill the kettle with snow, we could get some hot water to bathe your blistered heel,' the young man said in a tentative sort of fashion.

'That's an idea,' she admitted.

'My name is Andrew Blackwood,' he said, 'and I'm on my way to the wedding of my best

friend, Adam Cormack, whose bride lives in
Thorwick. Why people who live in such remote
places should choose to get married in winter
is a mystery.' He sighed and then noted
with astonishment that her eyes had suddenly
become like stars, and there was an excited
look on her face.

'But how wonderful!' she cried. '*I'm* on
my way to that wedding, too! I'm Margaret
Dunnet's friend, and I'm to be one of the
bridesmaids.' She paused—both were silent,
paying tribute to that wonderful thing 'the
long arm of coincidence.'

When they recaptured their wits (which she
did first) there followed a spate of talk, and of
course, with mutual friends like the bride and
bridegroom, they felt as if they were old friends
too, and Barbara told him her name.

'Now,' she said at last, 'please *do* go and look
for the keeper's house. I'll bathe my foot when
you're away. I must be able to dance at
Margaret's wedding.'

'Please keep the first dance, and ever so
many more for me,' cried Andrew Blackwood,
who was considered by his friends a hopelessly
shy bachelor. They'd have got the shock of
their lives if they could have heard him!
But there was white magic in the air to-night

and it makes folk do daft things—things they'd never dream of doing in ordinary circumstances.

'I'll bring more peats,' he said, 'and I'll try not to be long away.' Evidently he did not know how quickly peats burn, for the supply he brought would not last very long. Never mind —once she got rid of him she'd hop to the lean-to and see if she could find fuel of some sort, and with a basin of hot water she'd doctor this aching foot of hers. Bother the thing, how it throbbed!

'You're sure you won't be lonely, Miss Murray?' he asked.

'No, not at all, Mr. Blackwood.' (You see how polite they were to each other.) 'The moon will be up presently, and I don't suppose I shall have any callers.'

Then he was gone—Barbara listened to his receding footsteps, and then hopping on one leg she proceeded to deal with that aching foot of hers.

The world seemed full of silence—full to the very brim. She could see through the broken door, the stars throbbing whitely in the dark sky, and presently the moon sailed into her line of vision.

The hot water soothed not only her foot but her nerves; the fire lapped cosily on the hearth;

she leaned her arms on the table, her head on her arms, closed her eyes and—fell asleep.

When she opened her eyes again she found sitting opposite her and watching her intently a strange-looking woman.

She was a queer, elfin-looking creature, with great black eyes, peering fearfully out of a lividly white face. Her lank black hair fell in wisps over her brow, and intensified the uncanniness of her appearance. Her ragged dress of faded tartan and her ragged shawl had the weather-beaten appearance of being out summer and winter; she wore heavy boots, and her stockings were thick, grey, home-knitted ones, and were the only comfortable-looking things about her.

Finding Barbara awake, this queer visitor poured out a torrent of vehement Gaelic, quickly and incoherently. She had a nervous way of jerking the hair out of her eyes with a toss of the head like a child, but her distressed eyes told that Shenag Macleod and childhood were sundered by unfordable rivers—uncharted seas!

CHAPTER 2

NURSE FRASER

ANDREW BLACKWOOD had not gone far when he realized that it was to be a difficult business to find the gamekeeper's house, even if the moor was flat. A countryman would have recognized direction-signs where Andrew saw only snow and rocks.

He thought uneasily of the girl he had left in the bothy; she was a brave lass, still a winter night is long and lonely when one is miles away from any other human being.

Now, where on earth was that house?

He climbed to the top of a hillock—away to the south he could glimpse the telegraph-poles which marked where the railway ran; that was one point fixed anyway. Supposing he tried this way—to the right? Malcolm the guard had pointed to the right; so on and on he stumbled, often feeling like a man in a dream and wondering why he, Andrew Blackwood, analytical chemist in the University of Manchester, was wandering about on a snowy moor carrying a can of milk and a bag of eggs, searching for the house of a sick gamekeeper whom he had never seen, and having left behind him in a roadman's bothy a girl who, till to-night, was a stranger. Remembering all this, he marvelled at himself—however, he was not angry! No. But he was surprised.

He stood still and sniffed. Wafted on the icy air was a smell—strange to him till that night—but which he now recognized as the smell of a peat fire. It was a scent, heartsome and cheery, and guided by it he toiled on. From the rising ground beside a frozen burn he saw the welcome light of a house. The world wasn't empty after all! There were houses in it, with people living in them and cosy fires and bright lamps. Cheers!

He squared his shoulders, shifted that truly annoying milk-can from his right hand to his left, and set out in the direction of the light. He'd get help for Barbara Murray—he repeated the name to himself—and decided he liked the sound of it. It suited her and her plucky ways, for she was plucky; yes, decidedly, Barbara was just the sporting kind of girl with whom to share an adventure.

Drat! There he was down again for the umpteenth time. He felt his pocket in which were the long-suffering eggs. 'Another egg

25

gone, I'm afraid,' he groaned, and stumbled on.

The barking of angry dogs told him that at last he was near the kennels and the house. In the still night air the noise they made was deafening. Presently the house-door was opened, and a cautious voice asked, 'Is anyone there?'

'Be quiet, you brutes,' Andrew muttered, and then, raising his voice so as to be heard, he said, 'Yes, a messenger sent by Malcolm Maciver the guard.'

By this time he was standing at the door.

'Be coming in, if you please, sir,' the woman said gently, 'and what message did you get from Malcolm?' She led the way into the kitchen, where a glorious fire of peats gave him welcome.

Andrew laid down the can of milk. 'There are eggs, too, but I'm afraid that two of them have come to grief,' he said, and drew a somewhat wet-looking parcel out of his coat-pocket.

'Now, surely it was the Lord that sent you,' Merran Macphail said in grateful tones, 'for didn't the doctor say to be giving Hector milk and eggs. The cows they are dry since September, and the very hens forget what like an egg looks. Sit you down, sir, and you'll taste.'

She bustled about from cupboard to table, bringing out oatcakes and cheese, and refusing to listen to her visitor's protests.

'It's grand stuff, it'll be doing you good,' she said, 'and after coming all that way from the station you'll be needing it. Be taking it, if you please, and I must tell the nurse what you have brought us.'

The ben-end door opened softly, and the figure of a nurse appeared. She nodded in friendly fashion, as Merran explained who was her visitor. 'I'll switch up an egg,' she whispered. 'You might warm a cup of milk. I think Hector's needing something to strengthen him, he seems weak-like just now.'

The two women moved quietly about. Andrew was thankful to see four whole eggs emerging from the bag.

'How's your patient, nurse?' he asked, and she said he was holding his own. Andrew had never seen the man, never even heard his name till a few hours ago, yet he had a deep interest in him for 'we live in deeds, not words.'

If I were a poet (which I'm not) I'd sing a pæan of praise to the District Nurse who comes to us in our dark hours and brings us help and cheer. The moment she enters the house—hangs up her navy-blue coat and cap on the back of the door and says, 'Where is the patient?' we feel as if the burden of anxiety has been shifted from our shoulders to hers. We had been asking God to send us an angel; so He did, and lo, she wore the uniform of a District Nurse and said of the patient, 'He's holding his own.'

Andrew Blackwood had never come into contact with a District Nurse till that night, and it says much for the strong personality of Nurse Mary Fraser that presently he found himself telling of his fellow-traveller whom he had left in the bothy nursing a hurt heel.

'But you were miles off your way if you were in the roadman's bothy,' she said. 'Yes, Merran, I'll take the milk now.' She slipped away, and when she returned with the report that Hector had enjoyed the hot drink, she also took up the conversation where they had left it.

Andrew tried to explain first how the train had stuck miles away from the station, how the engine-driver had feared that Hector might need the milk and eggs, and how he and his fellow-passenger had volunteered to deliver them.

Nurse Fraser asked a few questions about the girl he had left in the bothy. She seemed to think over something very carefully, and when she spoke it was to say that Hector was now much easier and would probably sleep and she'd accompany Mr. Blackwood back to the bothy and do something for the lady's foot.

'Will the leddy be your wife, if you please?' Merran asked politely, and was answered by the vivid blush which mounted to the young man's face. She nodded; clearly she thought if the lady wasn't his wife she was his sweetheart. Well, there was no time to explain.

Nurse Fraser had buttoned herself into her coat, and wound a scarf round her head and neck, and she had her black bag in her hand. 'Come on,' she said, as one who is in command, as indeed she was.

Merran, with many apologies for the liberty she was taking and for the poorness of the fare, handed to Andrew a parcel of oatcakes and cheese 'for the poor young leddy' and off they went once more. It seemed to the man that all his life he had done nothing but stumble over snowy moors, looking for people and houses which were no sooner found than they were lost again! Truly a memorable night.

Nurse Fraser was a stalwart lass from Aberdeen, and had much to say about her native city as they trudged along. She had a keen eye for the funny side of life, and made her companion laugh as she told him of the last case she had been nursing—a baby case. An old woman had come to ask for mother and child. 'Will the bairnie live?' asked the old woman. Nurse said, 'Oh yes.' The old woman pondered this, and then said, 'I hope it will, for they're telling me it was an *amateur* baby, an' they're aye hard tae rear.'

But the folk here were the kindest you could ever wish to meet. How had she reached Hector Macphail's house? Oh, the butcher had taken her in his van to the cross-roads at Bridgend, and there she had met Hugh the rabbit-trapper on his motor bike and he had taken her as far as Craigroy, and after that she had just got along by herself. No, it wasn't the length of the road that bothered her, but the slipperiness of it. She chuckled, 'I'm black and blue with falling, but thank goodness no one saw me.' It seemed a strange cause for thankfulness.

The moon shone down on a world of dazzling white; the beauty and solemnity of it were awesome, so that one did not wish to speak.

The busy, bustling world of everyday affairs seemed like a far-off dream to Andrew Blackwood. Nurse sensed it, too, for they both walked along in silence. Then she said, 'We should see the light of the bothy now. Look farther up. Can you see another little house?'

He could not.

'You see the bothy?'

'Y-yes.'

'Well, follow a straight line till you see a thing that looks like a snowdrift.'

He had located it now. 'I see it. Yes, there's a faint light there, isn't there?'

'There is,' she said grimly, 'and that means that Shenag Macleod is out roaming and her poor old mother is sitting waiting till she comes home. The poor old creature is so bad with rheumatism she can't walk any distance, as fine does Shenag know.'

'But who is Shenag?'

'She's a poor daft creature that wanders all over the glen. Her mother and herself came from the Outer Isles, where her father was a weaver. He's dead long ago. There's no harm in Shenag, but when the boys tease her she's like a wild thing—some trouble she had in her young days has left her queer.'

Andrew was thankful to see the light was

still burning in the bothy. Perhaps, with a bit of luck they might get back to ordinary life and civilization, and meals and fires some time soon. But to-night's experiences had not been without their pleasant side.

CHAPTER 3

SHENAG

BARBARA, still half asleep, and muddle-headed, gazed at the uncanny creature sitting opposite her. No, she was not frightened, but startled. One cannot entirely blame her either!

Shenag continued to speak rapidly in Gaelic, and then she asked a question in English. It was, 'And haff you the Gaelic?'

'I have not,' Barbara answered, 'and I wish you'd tell me who you are and why you've come here, and what's your name.'

'The name that's on me is Shenag,' the woman answered, 'and the boys are at me—they are throwing stones at me and snowballs. Look!'

She bent her head, and showed Barbara an ugly gash on her temple.

Barbara rose in distress. 'You must let me bathe it,' she said, hopping about. 'I've warm water in the kettle, and here is a basin.'

Shenag smiled gratefully; she did not understand what the stranger said, but she did understand her kind voice, her gentle eyes.

c   33

Using her handkerchief as a sponge, Barbara bathed the ugly wound. 'Does that hurt?' she asked, feeling Shenag writhing with the pain. She said something in Gaelic, but kept her head steady. There was in her eyes the dumb endurance one sometimes sees in the eyes of an ill-used dog, and Barbara's heart was touched. She was also greatly perplexed as to what to use for a bandage. The wound was a deep one, and should have been cleaned with some antiseptic.

Barbara was wearing round her neck a gaily-striped scarf. 'Needs must,' she murmured to herself, as she took this off and wound it turban fashion round Shenag's black head, using a strip of her wet handkerchief as a pad.

The poor, demented creature broke into little cries of delight and joy—she loved bright colours, and this scarf was like a yard cut off the end of a rainbow. 'Bonny, bonny,' she cried, and patted her own head, and then Barbara's hands. 'Thank you, thank you.' There was no doubt as to her gratitude, though there might be as to her words.

She rocked herself to and fro in a perfect frenzy of pleasure—her moods changed as quickly as the wind. Suddenly she remembered something. In her poor, disordered brain the

34

thought had arisen that she might give something to this kind lady.

Fumbling in some mysterious fold of her dress she drew out a sprig of heather—white bell heather—so wonderfully dried it looked as though it were just newly gathered; its waxen flowers had on them still the sheen of their youth.

'It is for good luck,' she said, and pressed the sprig into Barbara's hands.

At that very moment the half-open bothy door was pushed wide open, and two greatly amazed travellers looked in at the sight of a woman with her head tied up in a coloured scarf presenting something to another woman who, like 'Diddle-diddle-dumpling, my son John,' had 'one shoe off and one shoe on.'

Nurse Fraser was the first to speak. 'Shenag, what *are* you doing here? No wonder your mother has the light burning in the window. Be off home with you now—there's a good lass. Yes, yes, I see you've got a new scarf—it's bonny.'

'Bonny,' Shenag echoed, and rose to slip away. At the door she said something which two of her hearers could not understand (not having the Gaelic). Nurse, who understood but could not speak it, said Shenag had invoked the blessings of the Supreme Being upon the kind lady; Nurse smiled to herself—clearly she had not told them *all* Shenag had said as she took her departure.

When she went, Andrew explained to Barbara how with great good luck and Nurse's kind heart he had been able to bring her assistance.

'Let me see the heel,' Nurse said, turning to her new patient, and Andrew Blackwood, murmuring something about getting a further supply of fuel, slipped away.

Nurse examined the heel, explaining at the same time all about Shenag. 'But why did you give her your scarf?' she asked. 'Believe me, you'll need it this wild night.'

'I had nothing for a bandage,' Barbara laughed, 'and the poor thing has an ugly gash on her temple.'

'Humph,' Nurse muttered, busy with the blistered heel. 'Does that hurt you? Just for a moment, then! Aye, when I'm done with you I'd better go and have a look at Shenag's head. I might even get back your scarf from her. A bandage and a bit of boracic lint may not look so bonny, but they would answer just as well as the scarf.' This was said with awful sarcasm. Barbara agreed, and said humbly she had nothing else, but on *no* account was

Shenag to return the scarf; she was quite fiercely determined on this point.

'Is that more comfortable?' Nurse asked, and Barbara said it felt so good she'd dance or—better still—go to Shenag's cottage and see that her head was attended to.

'This seems to be my busy night,' Nurse said thoughtfully.

'By the way,' said a voice from the door, 'Mrs. Macphail gave me this for you, Miss Murray,' and he handed her the oatcakes and cheese.

'I'll eat them as I go along,' Barbara said, beginning forthwith on a crisp farl of oatcake.

'I think you'll stay and rest your foot,' Nurse said. She had taken an instant liking to these plucky strangers.

'She could lean on my arm.' Again it was a voice from the doorway, and there was in it an eager note. 'I could even carry her bits of the way on my back.'

Barbara laughed gaily, her mouth full. 'I'd bite your ear if you did,' she said. 'Forward march, by the left,' and she limped forth into the white night. Fortunately they had not far to go.

They will never forget the sight which greeted their eyes when they reached Shenag's home. The house, if one could call it such, was what is known in the Highlands as 'a black house,' circular in shape, with a fireplace in the middle of the floor. A hole in the roof, with an old bottomless barrel by way of a chimney, let out the smoke. A great fire of peats was blazing on the hearth, over which hung a three-legged pot, and on one side of the hearth sat Shenag's mother, a spinning-wheel before her, a basket full of 'cairded' wool by her side. Shafts of light from the fire danced on the black, sooty roof, and on the shining dishes on the dresser —but the old crusie lamp stuck into the wall did little more than make darkness visible.

Gaelic is essentially the language of love and of war, and there was no doubt about it—war had it at the moment! On a creepie stool before her sat Shenag, a pitiful, cowed-looking creature, with tears streaming down her face, and her hair in wildest disorder. Evidently her mother had torn the scarf off her head, while she scolded her.

'Now, now, what's all this?' Nurse asked briskly, taking, as usual, command of the situation.

Shenag's mother, Mrs. Macleod, rose when she saw her visitors. She could speak English. She said so herself.

'And is it yourself, Nurse? Yes, yes, I'm scolding Shenag here for wandering about the country when she should be in her bed, and now she's coming home telling me the boys were at her and that some kind leddy gave her this bonny scarf. All lies!' She spat out a Gaelic word.

'No, no, it's not lies,' Barbara said, coming into the circle of firelight. 'I gave her the scarf, and please do allow her to keep it. She didn't ask for it, I gave it to her, because I had nothing else to bandage her head with.'

'And what is wrong with her head?' the mother asked, in a hoity-toity voice.

Nurse, who had been examining Shenag's wound, answered, 'She must have got a sore blow on the head, and it's beginning to fester. Wait, Shenag . . .' and once more Nurse dived into her useful black bag. Mrs. Macleod was immediately contrite, and plunged into incoherent apologies to her visitors. The boys in the glen were no better than *rotten tots*, she said, and the way they were *conternally* at poor Shenag was a fair scunner!

Yes, she earned a few pennies by spinning, she said, in reply to a question from Barbara. She could dye, too, and she nodded towards the pot swinging over the fire, which evidently

39

held dye. 'But to make a good dye took a long time and no one is caring for home-made dyes nowadays,' she mourned.

'Oh yes, they are,' Barbara said eagerly. 'The company I work for are very anxious to get hold of good dyes made from *crottle* and seaweed and broom.'

The old woman gave a wise smile. 'There's more than *crottle* and seaweed and broom needed to make a fast dye,' she said cryptically.

She rose and hobbled to a kist in the corner of the house, and after rummaging about in its contents she brought out a bundle of clews (balls of wool) that looked exactly like a bunch of coloured balloons, only much more substantial and much more beautiful.

'See to them, now,' she said, in proud tones. 'Myself dyed them, but the dye is a secret.'

Barbara gave a little gasp of pleasure. Here in this most unlikely place she had stumbled, literally stumbled, on something for which she had long been searching—home-made dyes with a clearness in their colouring which no aniline dye can ever hope to have—the blue, the heavenly blue especially—made her give another gasp of sheer delight.

'Have you more?' she asked eagerly.

Mrs. Macleod rummaged in her kist again,

and this time she took out a Fair Isle jumper—
a garment glowing with colour and rich in
design beyond anything Barbara had ever
handled.

'This belonged to my man. I knitted it for
him—for the Sabbath days—years ago.'

'Do you still remember the way?'

The woman smiled. 'What you learn young
you never forget.'

'If you'll make a jumper like this, and with
wool you dye yourself, I'll buy it from you,'
Barbara said. 'I'll buy as many as you choose
to knit, and I'll pay you for them.' She named
a sum which to a woman accustomed to
counting her wealth by pennies and half-
pennies seemed like a dream.

'I'll come back and collect what you've
done,' Barbara said, and opening her purse she
paid a first instalment. This did more than
her words to convince the old body of the reality
of her proposal.

Andrew Blackwood, who seemed to be
specially good at keeping himself out of sight
till he was needed, now stepped forward. He
glanced with interest at the balls of wool,
and with a courteous 'May I?' he examined
very carefully the old woman's work. Then
suddenly he raised his head, and seemed to

listen. 'Isn't that the engine *tooting*?' he asked.
'If so, we'd better go.'

Barbara shook hands warmly with the old
woman. Shenag followed her to the door, her
eyes wistful. 'I'm coming back, Shenag,'
Barbara whispered.

Barbara gave a contented sigh when they
got outside, and taking an arm of each of her
companions said, 'Yes, it has been a fairly
stirring night, with one thing after another,
but no one can complain it was dull.'

The good folks of Thorwick were sitting
down to breakfast when the snow-stayed train
from Inverness, with snow up to its eyebrows,
puffed into the station. Out of it stepped two
weary-looking travellers. It was to be noticed
that both came out of the same carriage, which
was a third-class one. They had had to spend
the second night in the Station Inn at Duncairn,
where the innkeeper's wife fed them on hare
soup and venison collops. The wedding was
over—the bride and bridegroom had taken an
aeroplane to Inverness—'I'll never come again
to Meg's wedding,' Barbara said ruefully.
Mrs. Dunnet, Meg's mother, laughed, and
said, 'I hope Meg won't have another wedding!'

CHAPTER 4

A LETTER

LETTER from Barbara Murray, Secretary to 'Scottish Homespun Wool and Tweed, London,' to Rev. Hugh Macgregor, Minister of St. Bennet's Church, Abergower:—

> 'ST. NINIAN'S SQUARE,
> 'THORWICK,
> 'December 13, 19—.

'HUGH, MY LAMB,

'I take pleasure in sitting down to pen you these few lines, hoping this finds you as it leaves me, with a blister on my right heel and a bruise on my left.

'Do you remember the lady in *Cranford* who "was indisposed with a sprained ankle which incapacitated her from holding a pen?" And do you know it's quite true, for when your feet go on strike your hands do too—at least mine do. This and the snowstorm and Meg's wedding must be my excuses for not answering your last letter sooner.

'I was pleased to find it waiting me when I got here after a terrible journey north. We took hours and hours—two days, in fact—coming from Inverness to Thorwick. Listen to my tale!

'You know I meant to attend Meg Dunnet's wedding on Tuesday, and then carry on and do a spot of work for my firm (and very nice, too. See how diligent I am).

'It was snowing all the way from Edinburgh, but

by the time we reached Inverness the snow was coming down in icy flakes and the flakes organized themselves, as the railway guard said, and defied us. "We're staying here," said they. All the same, our train pushed on, dropping passengers along the line, till by the time the disaster happened there were only two of us left—another and me.

'The "other" was a superior-looking young man. When I say he travelled first-class perhaps it is unnecessary to state he looked like a Greek god, and he was clad in an expensive-looking coat and wore fur-lined gloves, and had an opulent-looking suitcase with the initials "A.B." embossed on it, and a silk umbrella. I just got a glimpse of him as I passed along the corridor to my humble place in the third-class, with my shabby suitcase in one hand and in my other a cardboard box in which were the glad rags I meant to wear at Meg's wedding.

'The train dashed along with the hot haste peculiar to the Highland Railway, but in the midst of a snowy moor and with drifts as high as the engine, the train gave up the ghost. He (or is it she?) folded his hands, sat down on the line. "I can go no farther" were the words uttered.

'The railway guard, a cheerful-looking old buccaneer with red whiskers and a hilarious air, who seemed to think the whole thing a joke, advised us to descend. It was going to take *hours* to get the train going again; why, the very water in the engine threatened to go off the boil! He told us there was a gamekeeper's house "a mile and a bittock off" where we might get shelter. He also gave us a can of milk and a paper bag of eggs to carry to the keeper, who was ill in bed.

'My dear Hugh, let me advise you never to go for

44

a walk over a frozen moor, carrying eggs in a paper baggie, though I must confess I cannot imagine the dignified Hugh Macgregor ever carrying eggs either in a cardboard carton or in a bag.

'The superior young man didn't like it either, but off we set. The "bittock" extended to ten or twelve miles! And we ended by getting lost and taking refuge in a roadman's bothy, and by this time I developed a blister on my heel—I also managed to break an egg.

'A raw, broken egg is about as unpleasant-looking an object as one can see. Shipwrecked mariners and arctic explorers would no doubt have swallowed it. We did not—we threw it away. My mind was dwelling on succulent things like steak and onions.

'There was a store of peats in the bothy and we started a fire, and when we were doing it we discovered we were both going to the same marriage—namely, Margaret Dunnet's. He to be best man, if you please!

'So, of course, we got "pally" after this. His name is Andrew Blackwood, and he does something mysterious about dyeing in a textile factory in Manchester. Perhaps I haven't got the facts right —he was a little vague; and, anyway, he was all of a dither to deliver the milk and eggs at the game-keeper's.

'I suggested he should go by himself, and told him about the blister, whereupon he became very conscience-stricken, and filled the kettle with snow and fetched a basin, and brought peats for the fire, and altogether "came out strong" like Mark Tapley.

'After he left I had another adventure; a daft-looking woman slipped in. I was a little scared, but she showed me a terrible gash on her head, and I forgot to be frightened. To make a long story short, we went to this creature's home and there I found what I've long been looking for—a woman who's deeply versed in all the mysteries of home dyes. She was the mother of my visitor and she showed me some wools she had dyed herself, and the colours, my dear, were unbelievable. I made a bargain with her, if she'd knit jumpers for me I'd pay her, and she agreed. I'd like to find out about the dyes. I'd also like to find out about a sprig of white bell heather which her daughter Shenag gave me. The heather was as fresh as the day it was gathered.

'We were a day late for the wedding, of course—everything was over when we reached Thorwick, on Wednesday. Address your next letter to the Post Office, Inverbay, Kyle of Lochalsh. I expect you're busy with your Bible Class and your Sunday School Christmas Tree, but please write to your wandering but loving,

'Babs.'

'PS.—Do you remember Molly Swanson, who took the maths. class with us when we were in Aberdeen University? I met her in Thorwick, as small and quiet and mousy as ever. She teaches higher maths. in the Girls' School and spoke of you in a *reverent* tone of voice!—B.'

CHAPTER 5

ON HER ROUNDS

MAIRI MATHESON was spinning. She was sitting on a low chair by the hearth, and the peat fire threw flashes of light on the shining spokes of her spinning-wheel; then it danced on the brass pendulum of the solemn old wag-at-the-wa' clock, it flashed on the pewter plates standing like soldiers on the au'mory, and made of the unlighted lamp on the table a thing of curious iridescence. Soon she would have to light it, for the short winter afternoon was drawing to a close.

The song of the spinning-wheel is one of quiet content, and in the present case it formed a soothing accompaniment to the purring of Laorag—Mairi's black tom-cat—who, having dined sumptuously on a young rabbit, was feeling at peace with the whole world.

Deftly Mairi picked up the rolls of cairded wool one by one, and with her guiding hand on the spindle and her foot on the treadle she changed the fleecy roll into a thread—the thread became a clew. 'Tis an ancient occupation and one which lends itself to much thinking and brooding.

Who is to be the wearer of this wool, and how is life to fare with him or her? Someone is to be the better and the warmer, because of this work of the spinning-wheel; this is a pleasant thought.

Then a knock came to the door.

'Come in,' Mairi cried. That was the kind of woman Mairi Matheson was; she cried 'Come in' to all who knocked at her door, sure that her visitor was a friend.

She used, of course, the Gaelic equivalent of 'Come in,' and somehow to a Celt's ear it has a more welcoming sound than the English words—it implies that the speaker has been expecting and even longing for the visitor, and so 'Come in and welcome.'

And how warm was the welcome Barbara Murray got as she entered. Mairi rose to her feet at once, pushing aside her work—her face beaming and her hand outstretched.

'And is it yourself that's in it, *m'eudail*?' she asked. 'Wasn't myself thinking it was maybe Jess from the smiddy, or Merran Munro waiting here for Hughie-the-van—this is his day whatever. And it was yourself!'

She drew a comfortable chair nearer the

fire, built on more peats, shoo'ed the cat off the hearth-rug, and swung on the kettle.

Her movements, like her voice, were quiet and gentle, yet she managed to get through an incredible amount without the slightest fuss.

Barbara had made her acquaintance some time ago when she first came on her rounds collecting goods for her London firm, and the acquaintance ripened into warm and true friendship.

Mairi was a Celt, and no Celt is money-grubbing; so the business part of their trans-actions was always lifted by her into an affair of friendliness. She admitted Barbara into her world of thought, and gave her some-thing far more precious than mere material things.

She told her of 'boddachs' and ghosts; of folk with the 'second sight'; of the boobrie, and the each-uisge (water-horse). She let her into the thought world of the Celt—peopled with strange beings, whose presence in the glens and the rivers made life one long, high adventure!

Then quite suddenly Mairi would say, 'And I have here but twelve clews of wool for you this time, my dear. Didn't John-of-the ferry bring me wool, full of "burrs" and that

D

short in the grain myself could hardly caird it.' And she would bring out a bunch of balls of wool, and apologize profusely for their number.

'But these are beautiful,' Barbara would assure her.

'Not at all, not at all,' Mairi would reply, with a sad shake of her head, and would point out to this and to that defect in the spinning. But though she looked serious, she was quite glad that Barbara laughed and assured her she couldn't see anything wrong with the balls.

But on this cold winter afternoon the talk was all about the snowstorm, and Barbara related her adventures in the snow-bound train. She told Mairi about the strange couple whom she had met on the moor— Shenag and her mother.

'I'm knowing who they are,' Mairi said. 'They are from the Lews. Macleod will be the name that's on them.'

'Yes, but how did you know?'

'My father was a catechist in the Lews, and he used to be speaking about them. The man was a weaver (breabadair), and they were saying that his wife was akin to the good folk, and got from them the secrets of dyeing—and

that is why her lassie is queer in the head—
she's a changeling, and knows strange things
about flowers.'

'She knows how to preserve bell heather,
so that months after it is picked it looks as
fresh as when it was gathered,' Barbara said.
The other woman nodded thoughtfully; she
had more to tell, but not just now. She
turned her attention to the kettle, which had
begun to boil.

She made no apologies for entertaining her
visitor in the kitchen; in fact, had she laid the
tea in the 'ben-end' it would have been a
sign that she and Barbara were mere chilly
acquaintances. When Barbara had been on
her first rounds she had had tea there, and had
disliked its starched and stiff appearance, and
had begged to be allowed 'but' where there
were fire and friendliness, a 'creepie' by the
hearth, and a purring cat to nurse!

Bannocks and blaeberry jam—that was the
fare Mairi brought forth for her visitor. Tea
bubbling excitedly out of the spout of a little
brown teapot had to be drunk 'black'; the
cows were all dry, 'and look, see you, not one
drop of milk will I have till Bluebell calves in
March.'

City-dwellers have a pleasant belief that

milk, cream and eggs are to be had all the
year round in the country—alas, quite an
erroneous belief, for it is much easier to get
these commodities in the city than in remote
country places where for months the only milk
to be had is from 'the tin cow,' the condensed
milk brought by Hughie-the-van. Until
poultry farming is done on more scientific
lines there will always be a dearth of eggs in
winter too. Hens lose their feathers in autumn
and make this an excuse for 'going off the lay'
for months.

The foreign market supplies the city; but
the country places—remote and Highland—are
badly catered for.

When Mairi mentioned all this, Barbara
laughed her into silence. 'Your tea always
tastes good,' she cried, 'and this blaeberry
jam is fit for a king.'

Over the teacups the talk swung from
snowstorms to spinning, and Barbara had to
see once more the new clews and to admire
a wonderful scarf which Mairi had knitted.

'It's for you—for your New Year gift,'
Mairi said, 'and into every stitch of it I knitted
a good wish and a prayer.'

Barbara was speechless. What *is* one to say
for such a royal gift?

'And I haven't a scarf in my possession at the moment,' she cried at last, in warm, grateful tones, wrapping the new one round her throat. But she did not tell she'd given her own one, the gaily-striped one, to a poor 'truaghan,' who had called it 'bonny, bonny.'

And so with much goodwill on either side, and a modest little heap of 'white pennies' on the end of Mairi's mantelpiece, those two parted. Tom-the-carrier would call and collect the clews the following day.

It is quite impossible to tell the difference it has made to hundreds of Highland women to have their work bought and paid for. Money! Why, some of them scarcely knew the colour of it, and now, thanks to Barbara Murray and the rest of her committee, it was possible to bring hard-working women money, of their own hand's winning—a glamorous and new experience where all the money that comes into the home is earned by the man. The old saying that 'a man earns the money and the wife spends it' is now only partly true, and for the first time in their lives women in lonely corners of the Highlands and Islands are experiencing this new delightful feeling of earning money as well as spending it.

The short winter day was drawing to a close

when Barbara returned to the hotel which she had made her headquarters when collecting tweeds and wools from her district in the Kyle of Lochalsh.

On her way back Barbara met old Farquhar Macleod from Glen Rory returning from the merchant's—a parcel of 'loaf bread' in one hand, a stout walking-stick in the other, a red 'nepkin' tied over his cap—whether for warmth or security Barbara never found out.

He was a cheery old chap, with a gay (if toothless) smile, and a joke for everyone he met. When he was younger he had been in the habit of going to the Navy every year for a period of practising. His adventures there were a never-failing source of entertainment. If his hearers looked incredulous he used to say to his wife Betsy, 'Isn't that true, Betsy?' and she, being both a truthful and a tactful woman, used to reply, ''Deed, Farquhar, many's the time I've heard you telling that same story.'

He was genuinely delighted to meet Barbara, whom he, and indeed all her clients, called 'the leddy from London.' Yes, it had been a stormy winter, but nothing to the storms he had known in his young days when he used to be in the Navy. Why, he had seen—'and, mind you, this is no' a word o' a lee'—he had seen such frosty weather that the cries of the seagulls were frozen as they flew, and fell like lumps of ice on the deck.

'It's as sure as death they'd be falling on the deck wi' a "plop", the poor craiturs.'

He asked Barbara of her journey northward, and sympathized with her, though her adventures were nothing compared with his. Why, he had been going to the town quite lately and he thought—'for, mind you, I'm not a man without courage'—he'd go in the bus instead of the train.

'It was just before the New Year,' he explained, 'an' Hersel' was needing one or two things for the occasion. I got to my journey's end and did my messages, an' had a few words wi' one or two o' my friends, an' what wi' one thing after another I was late in getting to the bus. All the seats in the down part were filled. "Ye'll need to go up the stair, Farquhar," says Geordie-the-driver. So up I went—it was not easy an' me carrying all yon parcels—an'—an'—things. There's something about the air o' the town that makes me dizzy in the head and weak in the legs, so I had to go up slow. . . . But I cam' doon quick! For, look you—there were seats, an' plenty o' them, upstairs . . . *but there was no driver!*' He paused to see if Barbara was duly impressed by this terrific adventure. She was! She even said that possibly in the Navy he had never had such a narrow escape.

Much gratified by this he went on, ''Deed I had a narrow escape, an' so had the rest o' them, for believe me the Most High must have been looking after them, for they reached the journey's end the very same time as the rest o' us, an' not a bit the worse though they had no driver. I'm taking home "loaf bread," for not a tooth have I in my head, an' I canna eat oatcakes.'

Barbara told him to tell his wife she'd be along next morning to collect her knitting, and in the best possible frame of mind they took their separate ways.

Away in the distance, the 'wine dark sea' between it and the mainland—lay the Island of Skye. The hills were still wearing their mantle of snow; on the low land near the sea the ground was black and lights twinkled on the fishing - boats riding at anchor in the harbour. Silence filled the world to its brim— the booming of the waves on the beach only seemed to accentuate it. Overhead the stars and a moon that looked like a 'galley of

Lorn' looked down at their own reflections in the water and said it was good.

Barbara stood drinking in the beauty of the scene till the coldness of her feet warned her it was time to return to the hotel. The thought of a fire, of a warm meal, and of a cosy chair, was very pleasant. Perhaps there might be letters, too? There might be one from Hugh. She quickened her pace at the thought of it.

A hasty examination of her letters showed there was none from Hugh. She sighed. Sometimes she wished Hugh were a more impetuous lover who would write her every day, which was of course absurd, but Barbara was rather an absurd person herself!

There were two letters with unfamiliar writing. She examined them carefully before opening them. The first was from Molly Swanson, and for some mysterious reason Barbara frowned when she glanced at the signature.

'What does Sly Boots want?' she asked herself, sure that Molly had some request to make—Molly being that kind of a girl!

Sure enough, Molly with many apologies was begging a favour. If Barbara would be so kind as to write to the Rev. Hugh Macgregor on her behalf she would be eternally grateful. She was applying for a post as teacher of higher maths. in the Girls' School at Abergower, and she understood the Rev. Hugh was a person of influence in the Educational Council. She didn't like to write to him herself, but if Barbara—whose word, of course, would have the greatest possible influence with Mr. Macgregor—would speak a few words on her behalf she'd get the post, which was one that carried a bigger salary than she had at present. 'And, you know, since Father died I am wage-earner——'

The frown had deepened into a scowl when Barbara reached this part of the letter. 'She would, of course, try to make me sorry for her,' she said wrathfully. 'Well, I'll be writing to Hugh to-night, and I'll mention the matter, though I hate asking favours for myself or anyone else.'

Then she turned her attention to the other letter. It was in 'a man's han' o' write,' firm and full of character. She opened it with interest, and glanced at the signature—'Your fellow-traveller—Andrew Blackwood.'

Barbara's eyes sparkled. 'And what have you to say for yourself, Andrew Blackwood?' she murmured.

The writer hadn't much to say; he hoped she was none the worse of her adventure in the snow, and that the blister on her heel was better. Might he ask as a great personal favour if she came across any new (or old) methods of dyeing from vegetables she would let him know. His firm would gladly pay for any such information, and their strange encounter with Shenag and her mother, and the sight of the balls of home-dyed wool, had set him speculating.

'Hoping he was not troubling her, and with best wishes for the New Year, he remained . . .'

Quite a business-like letter, one would think. Barbara said so, and she re-read it—she also read between the lines, and she may or may not have got more information from this. At any rate she laid the letter aside very carefully, and was, on the whole, rather pleased that she and Andrew Blackwood were not quite to be 'ships that pass in the night,' so long as there were letters. She mused pleasantly as she took her tea. Life was a queer, topsy-turvy affair. She had expected a letter from Hugh and had not got it; she certainly had not expected a letter from Andrew Blackwood, yet here it was! True, it was more or less of a business communication, all the same it was clear the young man hadn't forgotten their shared experiences in the snowstorm. And this is how she answered:

'*From* B. MURRAY

'*To* ANDREW BLACKWOOD, Esq.

'*January* 10, 193—.

'DEAR SIR,

'*Re* yours of January 5, I beg to state the contents noted, and when further communication is obtained, you shall be communicated with. Assuring you that everything in our power will be done to obtain the information desired,

'We are,

'Yours respectfully,

'*p*. Scottish Homespun Wool & Tweed,

'BARBARA MURRAY.

'PS.—You will note that in order to be business-like one must avoid simple statements like " I'll see what can be done about these dyes, and let you know," which is what I'm really trying to say.

'Yes, thank you, my heel is quite better; perhaps it was as well I hadn't that dance at Meg's wedding, though I was disappointed. I'm wandering around collecting my own wits and my cailleachs' (old wives) woollies—the former more difficult than the latter.

'Yours, still in a snowstorm,

'BARBARA MURRAY.'

She decided to wait till next day before writing to Hugh asking his help for Molly Swanson. Perhaps by that time she would be able to think more kindly of Molly, and to sympathize with her position as breadwinner. At the present moment she wanted to smack her nice smooth little mousy head, and to tell her to do her own 'axing'!

CHAPTER 6

A FAIR ISLE JUMPER

ONE of the houses to which Barbara liked to go was called 'Braighe,' which means 'The top of the glen.'

In it lived Uistean Maclennan, his wife Jess, and their children, and the old Granny known familiarly as 'Granny Clouston.'

As the name implies, Granny belonged to Shetland, and in a place like the Kyle, where Gaelic was the language of the fireside, the old woman often felt very lonely, for she knew not a word of it.

Neither did her daughter Jess, but she had been so deeply in love with Uistean that nothing else mattered. So the old woman, much against her will, had broken up her home in Shetland and had come to the 'Braighe' to keep Jess company when her man was away at the fishing, and then to act as nurse for the babies as they came along.

At first the arrangement had been a happy one, but now there was no blinking the fact that the 'Braighe' was too little to hold them all. And, worse still, Granny had fallen one slippery

winter day and had broken her leg, after which
she could only hobble painfully along. She
felt that she was not worth her house-room, and
it was a bitter thought and one she did not
dare to utter, for Jess and Uistean would have
been the first to deny it.

Barbara had stumbled across her one day
carrying a pail of water from the little well
and spilling quite half of it. 'I'll carry that,'
Barbara said, and took possession of the pail.

Granny Clouston protested vigorously. Barbara heeded not. Instead she said, 'I do like
to hear you speaking. I remember once
spending a holiday in Ollaberry——' She got
no further.

'Ollaberry?' Granny echoed, her eyes shining
with excitement. 'An' dost du know Ollaberry?
I was born dere.'

Then followed a flood of memories. They
sat down on a handy tussock of heather, and
the foundations of a real friendship were well
and truly laid between a homesick Shetland
exile and the 'leddy from London.'

Granny told more than she knew, as one is
apt to do on such occasions. It was so long
since she had had a heart-to-heart talk with
anyone, and, yes, she was lonely, and she was
homesick, too, but it wasn't Jess's fault, it wasn't

anybody's fault, and no one could help her but God, and He could only help her by taking her away.

'I am for no use now,' she said sadly.

'Don't say that,' Barbara cried, her eyes bright with unshed tears. This business of hers was bringing her up against the human problem and making her reckless. 'You can knit, all Shetlanders can. If you knit, I'll get you the wool, and I'll sell the garment too.'

It was a sporting offer, for remember, beyond the general fact that all Shetland women were good knitters, Barbara had no means of knowing if Granny Clouston was one of these or not. She didn't care—she must slay this awful idea of the old woman's that she was 'for no use.'

She knew that the power to create is one of the most rejuvenating things in the world—no beauty culture to compare with it.

Recklessly she dispatched to the old woman, when she returned to London, a bundle of rainbow-coloured wools. If now and then she had an uneasy moment as to the result, she stifled it.

And it must be confessed she had more than an uneasy moment—she had one of sheer panic—when she saw the result of her venture on her next visit to the 'Braighe.'

Jess had shown it to her, explaining that Granny was now so much better she was able to go to the merchant's to do the shopping.

There is an old saying, 'Fools and bairns should never see half-finished things,' and the sight of Granny Clouston's half-finished garment scared Barbara. It was shapeless—incredibly dirty—and hopelessly spoiled.

Granny must have worked at it while she went on her way to the stack for peats and to the well for water. She must, Barbara thought miserably, have used it as a floor mop and a duster. She had worked at it with dirty, grimy hands. It smelt of fish and oil. Barbara felt dismayed, for far more than the mere jumper was at stake.

'My mother wouldn't like to know you had seen it,' Jess said, and Barbara, making vague sounds, fled from the 'Braighe.'

'We'll send it by post,' Jess called after her.

The parcel, smelling of peat reek, arrived one morning in London when Barbara was unpacking wools and tweeds. She hoped no one was at hand to see, and she poked the peat-smelling parcel into a corner. Sometime, when she felt strong and brave, she'd open it.

That time arrived after lunch. She had fortified herself with a cup of strong coffee.

E

'Now for it,' she said, and with grim reckless-
ness she cut the many strings.

'I'll burn it, or I'll unwind it—I'll do
something with it,' she promised herself, as she
took off paper after paper. . . . And there . . .
she had to rub her eyes . . . yes . . . there was
Granny's Fair Isle—and never in all her
wanderings had she seen one so beautiful.

'It's a miracle,' she whispered, and opened
out the garment. The shape was perfect—the
sleeves, always a difficult part of a jumper, had
been grafted into the shoulders with cunning
stitches and wonderful designs. The patterns
—there were five of them—were intricate and
lovely, and the whole garment was as soft as
silk and as light as a feather. Yes, it was
undoubtedly a miracle.

And underneath was a Fair Isle cap, one of
those fascinating things so becoming to a girl's
face, ending in a tassel and, very clearly, it was
made from the tail of a rainbow. In carefully
spelt letters a note explained that this cap had
been made with the wool left over.

Perhaps some of my readers will recall how
that summer a certain Exalted Personage made
Fair Isle jumpers popular by wearing one herself
and with a cap to match. I am proud to tell
you that Barbara Murray's venture of faith

proved an overwhelming success, and there—
Granny Clouston—is the woman who justified
her venture! Incidentally, orders for Fair Isle
jumpers came pouring in, so now you understand why Barbara always looked forward to
her visit to the 'Braighe.' The sight of Granny's
cheery face was like a tonic.

When she called there the following morning
she found them busy over plans for building
an extra room to the house—oh, quite a small
room, but one for Granny's own use.

Barbara, knowing Granny's kind heart, was
pretty sure that the room would be shared by
one or two of the grandchildren. 'The love of
money is the root of all evil,' says Paul. Quite
often the want of it is the root of family quarrels
and misunderstandings.

'I'm knitting fur du, scarves and caps this
time,' Granny said, and brought out a bundle
as colourful as a garden in June. 'This is one
special—for *dursel*!'

'Speak about casting your bread on the
waters,' Barbara laughed, and told them she
had not a scarf in her possession when she
came to the Kyle, and now she had two—both
beauties, far lovelier ones than she had ever
before possessed.

'And little Jessie's learning to knit,' Granny

said proudly, 'and she's helping her ould Granny—see to dis now,' and she held out a piece of knitting. 'Garters,' she said laconically.

Barbara duly admired them, and then asked could Granny knit gloves.

Why, yes, of course.

Then here was an order for a dozen pairs of wrist-length ones, and a dozen pairs of elbow-length.

The old woman was hugely tickled at the thought of the London 'leddies' wearing the gloves she knitted. 'If dey but knew it was an ould wife like me,' she chuckled, 'an' if dey could but see da hoose!'

On the whole, Barbara was glad they could not. But how interesting was the human side of this business of hers.

CHAPTER 7

THE MANSE LADY

MRS. MACARTHUR and Meena, the maid of the manse, were folding sheets in the cosy kitchen which was full of the fragrance of linen dried in frosty weather and hot irons ready to smooth everything into loveliness.

'It's a blessing the washing dried in the forenoon, for the day is quite damp now and foggy,' Mrs. Macarthur said, 'and the sheets and table-cloths are just right for folding. Here, Meena, catch hold.'

They tugged the sheet into straight folds. 'Don't pull me off my feet now, Meena,' Mrs. Macarthur laughed, for Meena was a hefty lass and a muscular one to boot. 'Have you got the hem straight at your end?'

Meena said 'Yes, mem,' and then she cocked her head and seemed to listen. A footstep and a loud thump at the back door told her she wasn't wrong—there was someone there.

'It's Peter-the-paraffin,' she said. 'How much o' gallons are we needing?'

Mrs. Macarthur hastily finished the sheet-folding. 'Ten, Meena, and tell him not to spill

quite so much on the floor as he did last time,
and be *quick back.* I'd like the ironing done
before tea-time. I'll be getting on with the
ironing of the minister's hankies.'

Meena was out of the door like a shot.
Peter-the-paraffin didn't like to have to wait
at closed doors—he didn't mind if they were
open and a bonny lass stood on the threshold—
'argy-bargying' about the price of paraffin
and the sinful way he spilled a drop or two
when he measured it out.

Peter had a 'come-hither' look in his blue
eyes; he had, too, a 'way with him,' so that
every lass with whom he held parley got the
impression that she and she alone was the girl
of his heart! A rogue of a lad, but not without
redeeming qualities, 'for, look see, how good he
is to his old mother! Gives her her breakfast
in bed every morning, and makes ready the
meals for the two of them. It's as sure as you're
there; the poor laddie would be much the better
of a wife.' The lassies were all kindly concerned
over Peter's sad state.

Meantime Mrs. Macarthur, having tested the
box iron by holding it close to her cheek, was
smoothing the minister's hankies, and every
minister's wife knows how important it is that
these should be of a snowy whiteness. Every

right-minded wife is 'black affronted' if on a
Sabbath day the minister in the pulpit takes
out a hankie that is grey in colour and limp in
texture. If the husband of the virtuous woman
is known in the gates, the minister, by means of
his hankies, is known in the pulpit.

And the iron was just the proper heat to deal
with the damp linen and to give it the requisite
gloss and stiffness. She had finished the first
one and had begun on the second when the
front door bell shrilled.

'Mmmmm,' she said, and went on with her
work.

The bell shrilled again, more insistently than
the first time. She sighed, laid down her hot
iron, whipped off her cotton overall and went
to open the door, hoping as she did so that she
would not be kept too long away from her
ironing. She was an incurably optimistic
woman!

The lady who stood on the doorstep was
tall and stout and opulent-looking. Her fur
coat, her smart little hat, her large expensive handbag, all spoke the same language—
money!

She pulled off a fur-lined glove, and extended
a hand loaded with rings. She cried: 'We *do*
really know each other! I'm quite right! You

are little Alison Gray, the sweet little girl I
was in school with? And you've grown into a
sweet little woman, if you'll allow an old friend
say so.'

Mrs. Macarthur made strictly non-committal
noises, but she cordially disliked being called a
'sweet little woman.' It was almost as bad as
being called a 'dear wee soul.'

'Don't break my heart by saying you don't
remember me,' the visitor gushed. 'Charlotte
Beverley—you naughty things used to call me
Charlie.' She kept an eye hard in expression
and grey in colour fixed on the other's face as
she said these words.

Mrs. Macarthur had meantime been casting
her mind back to the days of her youth. Yes,
she did rather vaguely remember Charlotte
Beverley—an empty-headed, over-dressed girl,
the despair of her teachers. Why—wasn't she
the girl who had come to school one morning
resplendent in a black satin dress embroidered
with bunches of cherries, and with cherry-
coloured ribbons in her hair? She had been so
delighted with herself that she made innumer-
able journeys across the schoolroom in search
of articles which she said she had mislaid.
Miss Texel, the English teacher, a lady with a
nippy tongue and a bored manner, looked

calmly at Charlotte, and then said: 'You may sit down now, Charlotte, we have *all* seen you.'

Mrs. Macarthur smiled at the memory. Yes, yes, she remembered her now—a girl who was none too scrupulous about copying answers off her more brainy, if less wealthy, companions. Subconsciously she was asking herself: 'What does the woman want now?'

Meantime the visitor went on dauntlessly, 'I just said to my husband I'm *sure* the clergyman here is married to a dear old school chum of mine, and they are sure to help us. My name is now Mortimer-Smith.'

'Come in, please,' Mrs. Macarthur said, and cast a wistful thought to her fast cooling irons.

'Your husband is a clergyman?' Mrs. Mortimer-Smith went on.

'My husband is a minister of the Presbyterian Church of Scotland,' Mrs. Macarthur said solemnly.

'You quaint little creature! I wonder is it Calvin or the climate that makes us Scots folk speak of the "Presbyterian Church" and "ministers." Isn't there something sober and dour about the words? What a nice cosy room, and dear, dear, I am glad to see a fire.' She sat down on a comfortable chair as close to the hearth as she could get. 'It's my feet,' she said, in a confidential tone of voice, 'they get so cold.'

'Perhaps your shoes are too tight,' Mrs. Macarthur suggested, eyeing her visitor's high-heeled shoes.

Mrs. Mortimer-Smith took no notice of this remark. 'I hear your husband is a wonderful preacher,' she went on. 'Do you mind if I give the fire a wee poke? You know, I do know you for seven years. Isn't it only if one is a seven-year-old friend one is allowed to poke someone else's fire?'

Nothing could be more gushing than her words; nothing more drastic than the way she smashed a lump of coal which Mrs. Macarthur had been hoping would last the whole evening, coal being one of the most expensive items in a remote Highland manse.

Her guest, spreading herself, literally, opened her handbag and took out a cigarette case which she offered to her hostess, who refused it. 'I suppose you think I'm very naughty,' she said, 'but a cigarette is as necessary to me as a cup of tea to the rest of my non-smoking sex. And I haven't had tea yet.'

Mrs. Macarthur was only human. She didn't like her visitor; she still had to find out what she wanted (besides tea), so excusing herself she went to the kitchen to instruct Meena to make tea.

Meena was smoothing her hair and straightening her cap. Her cheeks were rosy, her eyes bright. The cold air, she explained.

Mrs. Mortimer-Smith made an excellent meal; she went out for her husband, whom she had left sitting in the car, and who was also cold and hungry. 'And if you don't mind, *could* your maid give our chauffeur a cup of tea? I think it's such a pity to forget one's servants' comforts and only look after one's own.'

Mrs. Macarthur agreed.

It was while 'an enjoyable time was being had by all' that Barbara Murray arrived.

CHAPTER 8

BARBARA had a happy, excited look on her
face, an apology on her lips, and a motor-rug
folded over her arm.

She greeted Mrs. Macarthur with a hug and
a kiss. 'But Meena did not tell me you were
engaged,' she said, glancing at Mrs. Mortimer-
Smith, who was carefully spreading butter and
jam on a scone.

Then followed introductions, and Barbara
found herself saying, 'How d'ye do?' to
this curious couple. Mrs. Mortimer-Smith
she summed up at once; she had not been
buying and selling for years without being
able to judge character. 'A human vulture,'
was her unspoken verdict on this large
lady who continued steadily eating and
drinking.

Mr. Mortimer-Smith was a neat, restrained-
looking little man, rather scant of hair, but
making the most of what he had. He had
round surprised-looking eyes rather like a scared
rabbit, and scared he undoubtedly was of his
large and well-upholstered wife. He was

'interested in wool' his wife said vaguely, 'and has mills in the Midlands.'

Mrs. Mortimer-Smith was just as busy summing up Barbara and trying to 'place' her. The newcomer's tweed suit was well worn, but it was of Harris tweed and had been fashioned by an expert tailor; her little sports hat could not have been bought under two guineas, and her shoes were neat, hand-sewn brogues. Yet she was collecting wools and tweeds for a London firm—ummmmm—a sort of glorified commercial traveller?

But it was Barbara who ran to the kitchen for a fresh supply of tea; she was either a very forward young woman, or a familiar friend in the manse; all the same, the tea she brought back was no better than tepid dishwater. On the whole, Mrs. Mortimer-Smith wasn't disposed to like Miss Barbara Murray. There was a certain strange expression in her eye as she poured out the tepid tea which required some explanation. No, *not* a nice girl!

At the same time Barbara told Mrs. Macarthur that 'Henny-from-the-Hill' was in the kitchen, 'asking if you have any of yon poultage stuff to put on little Johnnie's chest, for he was bad wi' the brown-kaddies again.'

She meant, Barbara supposed, antiphlogistin.

Mrs. Macarthur ran to fetch a can of this most useful medicine which has been a godsend to the woman who can't make a poultice.

Barbara meantime spread on the floor the motor-rug she had been carrying.

'What do you think of that?' she inquired proudly, and looked round to see what impression the rug had made upon the company.

'A beauty,' Mrs. Macarthur said in hushed tones.

'Rather nice,' quoth Mrs. Mortimer-Smith, licking her jammy fingers ere stretching forth her hand to examine the rug.

Barbara calmly moved the rug out of reach.

'Cat skins,' she explained, 'wild-cat skins! I got Mrs. Mactaggart, the old gamekeeper's widow, to cure the skins—she had learned the art from her husband long ago; then Flory and Sheila Mackenzie at the Lodge matched and sewed the skins—just look how beautifully they've done it! And all this matching of skins and making one piece fit into another had to be done from the back—the skins cut with old safety-razor blades, and the very thread used for sewing is a special kind of linen as fine as silk and as strong as wire; the green surround was made by Beanie Bain, who mounted the skins, and just look at the expert way she's mitred the corners. There you are, ladies—what offer for this unique and valuable motor-rug?'

'Is it for sale?' Mrs. Mortimer-Smith asked carelessly.

She was an immensely wealthy woman, but dearly loved a good bargain and would haggle like a fishwife over a penny hank of twine. The thought had occurred to her that here was a chance to acquire a cheap motor-rug of a very rare and beautiful kind. She could picture herself spreading it over the knees of Mrs. Ernest Rawson, for instance, when next she gave that uppish creature a lift in her motor-car. Mrs. Rawson had the temerity to call a mangy-looking fur rug which she possessed 'my buffalo robe.' It would be rather nice to give her a surprise with this new rug.

'I picked it up quite by accident in the Highlands,' she could picture herself saying. 'It *is* rather unique, isn't it? It's quite amazing what one can get in these remote places if one knows where to look.'

But the rug wasn't hers yet . . . she meant it to be, though.

'May I have a look at it?' she inquired sweetly. Barbara gave a swift look at her hands, and decided they were now free of jam, so held out the rug for inspection.

'Quite nice,' Mrs. Mortimer-Smith said in patronizing tones. 'I see this corner needs a few more stitches.'

This enraged Barbara. 'That's nothing,' she said sharply, 'just look at the way the skins are matched. You'll hardly detect the joinings, and, of course, the cat isn't really so long as this. There are really two skins in each strand of fur—ending with a head at one end and a tail at the other.'

'I suppose cat skins are very little value?'

Mrs. Macarthur, who had absolutely no business sense, replied: 'Oh, no—when my husband caught a wild cat stealing the chickens he shot it and threw its body into the burn. I think that's what generally happens.'

It would have afforded Barbara intense satisfaction to *shake* the lady of the manse. The woman had no sense, not a grain.

She glanced at Mrs. Mortimer-Smith and saw the predatory light in her eye.

'Then, seeing the skins are valueless, all one has to pay for is the trouble of curing and mounting them. The rug shouldn't cost very much.'

'This rug isn't for sale,' Barbara said thoughtfully. 'I was merely jesting when I asked "What offer?". Lady Langcroft of Northland has ordered this one, and I'm getting a motor-muff made to match.'

She allowed a minute or two for this piece of information to soak into Mrs. Mortimer-Smith's mind. Then she went on, 'I have a list of customers here, and of course it's going to take a long time to supply them all. Cat skins are very rare, and now that they can be used like this they will be becoming more and more valuable. So we must take our customers in rotation.' She consulted a list of names in her notebook. 'Yes, I see the Hon. Mrs. Strathoran is last on my list of twenty-five. I'm afraid, poor lady, she'll have to wait a bit.'

Mrs. Mortimer-Smith made a grab for her handbag. She asked her husband a question —evidently of some importance, for the man looked quite flurried and produced a fountain pen.

'Of course, we can't make all our rugs so large,' Barbara went on chattily, 'or we could supply you with a rug of this size but made of rabbit skins. They look really quite nice,' she went on, 'and are very much cheaper, only Lady Langcroft doesn't care for the homely bunny.'

'Neither do I,' snapped Mrs. Mortimer-Smith. She was opening her handbag and fumbling for her cheque-book; she had thrown discretion to the winds—she would possess this motor-rug (as supplied to titled ladies) or perish in the attempt.

'I'll write you out a cheque for the amount,' she said. 'I've taken rather a fancy to this rug.'

'Sorry,' Barbara said, and shook her head firmly.

'Oh, come now, Miss Murray,' an arch smile accompanied her words.

'I dare not disappoint Lady Langcroft.' Barbara hadn't enjoyed herself so much for ages. She folded up the rug and laid it—fur outward—on the sofa. She patted the fur, and ran her fingers through its silky pile. 'Lady Langcroft's mink coat will look ashamed of itself beside her new motor-rug,' she laughed. 'Well, Alison, I must be getting back to my hotel; there are letters to read and to answer. I must drop a note to Dorothy Langcroft telling her her rug is ready.'

'Tell her that you've sold the first rug to a woman who wouldn't take "No" for an answer.' Mrs. Mortimer-Smith was still arch; but she was also determined.

Barbara looked at her with sorrowful eyes.

'I'm really quite distressed about this, Mrs. Mortimer-Smith,' she said, 'but—but—you see—my difficulty—don't you?'

Mrs. Mortimer-Smith replied by rising from her seat, spreading the rug over her knees and saying with a proudly triumphant air: '*This is mine*—I refuse to part with it.'

The cheque she had to write out for it rather made her catch her breath (and Alison had said cat skins were cheap!) but Barbara did not refer to this. She seemed to think she'd done Mrs. Mortimer-Smith a great favour letting her have the rug. Doubtless when that lady came to think over the matter in the cool light of reason she'd feel justifiably annoyed. But not now—no, not now! She was triumphant.

She departed, hugging the rug to her bosom, and just remembered to say as she went out: 'Oh, Alison, do you think you could look out for nice comfortable summer quarters for us? I don't mind how plain the house is, provided there's a good kitchen range, plenty h. and c., comfortable clean beds, cosy chairs, good drains, and a garden where I could sit while Mr. Mortimer-Smith and the boys bathe, or boat, or fish. Did I tell you I have three riotous boys? I'll need four bedrooms and a maid's room—*you* know the kind of thing—just plain, clean, comfortable and *cheap*.'

Mrs. Macarthur promised to make out a suitable list, and the lady, accompanied by her small husband, to whom she now entrusted the rug, took her departure.

'You *wretch*,' Barbara said, turning to Mrs. Macarthur, 'why *did* you tell that shark of a woman cat skins are of no value?'

'But neither they are, Babs.'

'You'll never make a merchant, Alison Macarthur. Don't you know it's the law of supply and demand that makes things valuable or the reverse? And if there's to be a demand for cat-skin motor-rugs and muffs, of course the skins are valuable. Who is that unspeakable woman, anyway?'

'She and I used to go to the same school, but I had forgotten all about that.'

'So had she, I'm sure, till she found it convenient to remember to pay your manse a visit, sure of a good square meal and free information about summer quarters. You should charge the usual house agent's commission, Ailie.'

'You're a mercenary wretch,' Mrs. Macarthur said.

Barbara chuckled. 'I'm now returning to the hotel to report to my committee the first sale of the new motor-rugs.'

'And—and—Lady Langcroft?'

Barbara hooted with laughter. 'Dorothy Leslie as was? She's one of our committee, and as keen on her job as I am. She'll die of laughing when I tell her. And look here, Ailie, when you're sending the list of houses to that woman tell her to come back and see them, and I'll arrange to conduct her *personally* to all of them, and mind you choose houses with steep, rocky footpaths leading up to them, with a beautiful view, but without h. and c.'

It was that evening that Barbara, exhilarated by her encounter with Mrs. Mortimer-Smith, wrote a gay letter to Hugh Macgregor and reported her doings, and asked his help for Molly Swanson. She pondered over her day's work—the position of the lady of the manse was not without its drawbacks! Only, she'd be much more sensible than Alison Macarthur! All the same, she remembered with warm gratitude what this manse had been to her and what the friendship and helpfulness of the minister and his wife had done for her when she first came to the place. Yes, perhaps being a minister's wife was not so bad.

CHAPTER 9

STOLEN FROM THE POSTMAN

'SWEET BRIAR COTTAGE,
  'ARDCLACHAN, LOCHSIDE,
    '*February* 19, 19—.

'"DAWTIE,"

'There, Hugh, is a new Gaelic word. It has a nice meaning, too. If you don't know it, I'll tell it to you the next time I see you. I don't think I could put it down in cold black and white, for, believe it or not, I have my blate moments. So I'll whisper it in your ear when we meet.

'And this leads me to ask, "Are you coming to the Spring Exhibition?" You'll have finished your winter's work by that time, and you'll be all the better of a little holiday. Besides, isn't it time you bought a new kilt? Then you could give me the old one. I'd run a tuck in its hem—an elastic in its waist—and wear it like a proud young Chieftainess! *Do* come, Hughie boy! We have some most superior tweeds and tartans—dyed in the wool—handwoven —guaranteed not to shrink (see advt.), besides hose with really gorgeous tops.

'No, I'm not the least ashamed of myself for making that horrid Smith woman pay a decent price for her motor-rug. When you consider that the rug was really ear-marked for Lady Langcroft and that I only allowed Mrs. Smith to have it as a great favour, my only regret is that I didn't charge her more.

'Mrs. Macarthur who, poor lamb, has a conscience that bothers her worse than a nail in her shoe, was worried over the same matter. She and her husband, just to make up for it, cudgelled their brains thinking out lists of possible summer quarters for those bloated profiteers. I do hope the one they select will turn out to have a cracked kitchen range and a narrow footpath both steep and flinty leading up to its door. Yes—I—do—Hugh.

'Is that wrong? No, it's not, for they could and should pay a decent price. They, or rather she, wants accommodation equal to a first-class boarding-house to be paid for at the rate of a but-and-a-ben! And they've *pots* of money, too!

'A thousand thanks for being so good about Molly Swanson. She wrote me a gushing little letter of thanks. I expect the one she wrote you was even "gushinger," if there's such a word. I heard from Meg Dunnet's mother that Molly's father had left them quite well off—it was the thought of Molly being breadwinner that moved me to write you; however, I hope she'll be happy in her new post. She says she is so grateful to you that she'll do all in her power to help you in your church work. I always knew Molly had a zeal for good works.

'This is a wild spot, sunk in Celtic gloom, and having "for keeps" the depression from Iceland. But awfully nice people. My landlady is the local merchant and sells everything from post cards to prams, and including pigs, both sugar and pork. She is also the postmistress, and a more helpful and obliging woman you couldn't hope to meet. Her name is Rebecca, and as she came originally from Applecross she is known as Rebecca of Applecross, and her house is Sweet Briar Cottage. How's that for romance? I regret to state that despite the pretty name of the house, the chimney of my room refuses to "draw" on account of a family of starlings making

87

their nest in it for years and years. I, being a new-comer, had not the fortitude to dislodge these old tenants, so I wander into Rebecca's lovely clean kitchen and sit by her fire, and there I met the strangest little woman, Hugh! She's French and was once upon a time a lady's-maid to Lady Kilbran. Her mind gave way after a long illness, and Lady Kilbran, who has a kind heart, asked Rebecca to take her in as a paying guest.

'She's a thin little woman with restless, black eyes, and hands that flutter. She's dressed like a Jane Austen picture, and she's most particular about her appearance. When she's not "prinking" at the mirror she's making lace—bobbin lace—lovely stuff like cobwebs. I'm to get her to make some for our exhibition—after all, it'll only be a continuation of the "Auld Alliance."

'I came in dripping wet last night and she came fluttering to my side, helped me to wriggle out of wet garments and into dry ones, saying all the while, "You dear poor—you dear poor."

'Send your next letter to London, I hope to be there soon. The next time I come north I'm coming by motor—my own motor! How's that for swank? I'm so glad I can drive, although my brother Bob always declared I made the brakes scream in anguish. The car I'm getting is second-hand and has been donated to the firm by a kind-hearted member who wishes to show her appreciation of my work. Am I proud . . .? Oh no!

'I can't write more—my candle's down to its last drop of grease, and I've been writing with the hot-water bag in my lap. Please praise me, and excuse me too.

                      'Ever your loving wandering
                                            'Babs.'

'PS.—I'm glad I didn't close this letter last night, for the "depression from Iceland" has gone back to its home there. The sky's a lovely soft blue —the loch is sparkling—the air is balmy—and Rebecca of Applecross has given me a newly laid egg for breakfast. It's the *First Egg of the Season*, and the laying of it by a hen called Lady White caused as much excitement as did the laying of the foundation stone of St. Paul's in London—more, in fact!

'Fortified by this egg and by the lovely day, I've resolved to cross the Minch after all and collect the Harris tweed which I know is waiting for me in various villages. Quite a lot of the cailleachs (old women) in the Lews *weave* as well as spin.

'On my way to the bus stop—yes, there are buses here and rattling affairs they are, too!—I passed the little church and manse. The old minister has died and the church is vacant. The congregation are hearing candidates, and as everyone has a different choice, this is likely to be a long business. On the church door was nailed a notice which read as follows: "There will be no Lord's Day here next Sabbath as the minister expects to be at the bottom of the Loch." . . . As I was puzzling over this rather sinister notice, an old man came along—he was also waiting for the bus—and he explained that the service will be held in a little meeting-house built at the *end* of the Loch. I was really scared at first when I read the notice.

'This old man pointed out to me a long row of graves marked by crosses where a crew of foreign sailors—from Italy, I think—are buried. Their ship went to pieces one awful night, and everyone was drowned—there was just one survivor, a retriever dog belonging to the Captain, and it swam ashore

89

and was adopted by the old minister. I wonder how these strangers rest in the little Highland kirkyard —do they long for their own sunny homeland? Well, they couldn't rest among kinder folks than the Highlanders.

'And now, I'm really done. Please think kindly of "those in peril on the sea," especially the Minch, through which I shall be heaving to-night. I expect I shall bitterly regret having eaten that newly laid egg. I wave my hand to you.—B.

'PSS.—I've just been thinking about this vacant church, Hugh, and the poor folks who are like sheep without a shepherd. Why couldn't *you* come and be their pastor? From Rebecca of Applecross I can gather that the minister here would be a close personal friend, adviser, doctor and lawyer, and the people in return would give him their hearts' affection. After all, why should the cities of the south always get our young ministers? Think of it. And now, heave ho for the Minch! The wind is rising, too. Ugh!—B.'

'On Board the *Beltane Queen*,
'Bound for Stornoway,
'*February* 20, 19—.

'DEAR MR. BLACKWOOD,

'Many thanks for your letter. I am glad the very scant information, which was all I could glean, was of some use to you. I am on my way to the Island of Lewis, and am full of hopes that there I'll discover something about the vegetable dyes. Besides the plants (crottle, lichen, bent, etc.) used there are wild whirling words and incantations to be uttered over the dyeing pot.

'The *Beltane Queen* is heaving, so I'll retire to my berth. Do you remember those eggs we broke so recklessly that day we were wandering about in the snow? I've come to the sorrowful conclusion that's much the best thing one can do with them! You see, I've had a newly laid egg for breakfast this morning, and it's making a good deal of itself!

'I'll try to tell you about our London Exhibition later on, when my feet are on my native heath, although my name is not yet Macgregor, but——

'Yours sincerely,
'BARBARA MURRAY.'

The skies were weeping copiously when the *Beltane Queen* put in at Stornoway Harbour. Barbara tottered ashore, lifting her feet high, and feeling as if at any moment the ground might rise up and hit her in the face.

Next morning the rain continued as she set out on her rounds. There was one new client —an old weaver upon whom she wished to call. She had been told this old wife made wonderful tweed.

The motor-bus took her so far on her way, and 'Cherlie-the-driver' gave her minute directions for finding the house, which was 'Over the hill and across the burn and up a brae, and then you'll see it right in front of you, and be canny crossing the burn—there's yonder stepping-stones—ten of them—but if you would rather you could be crossing on the plank o' wood.'

She found the house, a little thatched 'half-house' overlooking the burn—a peat stack at one end, a byre at the other; and if you want to see a peat stack built on geometrical lines go to the Island of Lewis and you'll see it there.

The house door was closed. Barbara was in the act of knocking when a cry rang out, a child's frightened cry, so shrill it made her blood freeze. She stood still for a split second unable to move. The scream came again, more terrified than at first. Barbara opened the door and entered.

CHAPTER 10

THE WEAVER WIFE

THE door opened straight into a little kitchen.
On a chair by the hearth a fair-haired child
was sitting huddled up, her knees almost
touching her chin, her eyes full of terror, and
her two hands clutching her face.

Bending over her was a tall, gaunt, old
woman, holding in her hand a weapon of
some kind—it looked like a steel bodkin. Her
attitude was as threatening as the child's was
terrified.

'What are you doing to the child?' Barbara
cried, too angry to be afraid.

'*Beannich mise!*' (bless me), cried the old
wife, straightening her back to look at her
visitor, 'who's this?'

Both the child and the old woman gazed at
her in astonishment.

'What are you doing to the little girl?'
Barbara demanded.

'Little Iseaball? She has the toothache; she
can get no sleep day nor night with it, and her
mother—that's my daughter—sent her to me for
a cure. I gave her the cure of Saint Peter, the

disciple of Our Lord. I sewed it in the hem of her frock, and what, think you, did the wicked one do with it? Tore it out, and gave it to the other children in the school to make a laugh and a mock of the good man's charm.' She gazed reproachfully at little Iseaball, who wriggled uncomfortably.

'Then I made for her the charm of Michael the Strong—I said it over her, and her leaning on the trunk of a tree out yonder in the Glen. But that did not cure her. So now I'm trying a small piece of cotton-wool steeped in whisky, by your leave.'

She exhibited the weapon which had looked like a steel bodkin, and was, in fact, merely a knitting-needle on the point of which was the soaked cotton-wool.

'If she would allow me to put this in the hole in her rotten tooth, it would be doing good to her,' the old woman explained, 'but whenever I go near her she's giving *yon bawl*. You would think I was murdering her.'

Barbara smiled, but did not say that such had been her own thought. 'Suppose I would hold the little girl's hands, and promise her a penny if she'd keep her mouth open, do you think we could manage it?'

Whether it was the presence of a stranger or

the promise of a penny, one cannot tell; but the somewhat delicate operation was duly performed, and Iseaball told to keep her teeth clenched tight and then to spit out the whisky and the toothache, too.

After an anxious moment or two she announced: 'It's better, Granny.'

Barbara put a penny in her little hand, and with a smile on her face and a tartan shawl over her head, she ran home, her Granny calling out advice as to the spending of the penny. 'And mind, Iseaball *vocht* (poor), *no sweeties.*'

Then Barbara explained that she had come in search of home-spun tweed, and turned to the loom which occupied most of the room. She looked at a newly finished web which lay on it. In Skye, the majority of weavers are men, but in the Lews and the Outer Isles the weavers are women, and very beautiful is the work they do.

This web was of a small pattern, yellow and brown—the texture beautifully soft. It had, too, that curious woolly surface which made any garment fashioned out of it absolutely waterproof—a most important quality when one considers the moistness of the western isles.

The pattern is produced by crossing and twisting the different coloured threads. Red is for courage, green for youth, and blue for love. Then 'warp well the long threads, the bright threads, the strong threads; woof well the cross threads, to make the colour shine.'

The old weaver wife said, with an air of great candour: 'There are other things about the weaving,' but she did not specify what these other things were, for she was not to give away the secrets of her ancient occupation.

'The dye? Oh, the same dye gave both the yellow and the dark brown—it was just a matter of boiling for a long or a short time, and the crottle growing on rocks and trees was what they used for the dye. "Madder" gave both blue and purple, so did seaweed.'

'Green?' asked Barbara.

'Oh, that was the fairies' colour, and the dye was got from the heather. The fairies were not allowed to dye their garments yellow, for that was a colour got from the sun-god, with whom the fairies had no dealings. Green was for them, then; so were blue, and black, and red.'

Barbara asked the length of this web and the price. She found bargaining with the weaver wife was not a matter to be hurried over. How could it be when she had so much to say about fairies and all the mystic rites of dyeing cloth?

'What is the length of the web?' Barbara asked again. 'And what is the price per yard?'

The woman was vague. She didn't know, she couldn't say, and the price was just whatever the leddy from London was willing to give.

Barbara had met with cases like this before, and had her own way of dealing with them.

'I think, by the look of it, there are nineteen yards in the web,' she said.

'Begging your pardon, there's twenty-and-one. I'll measure to let you see.'

'And three shillings will be quite a good price.'

'There's a merchant from the mainland offering me four, and it's not a word of a lie.' She did not add that this merchant made it a condition to give her goods instead of money.

'I'll give you three-and-sixpence clean money,' Barbara said, producing her purse. A cheque, she had discovered, had not the same attraction for her clients as the sight of Treasury notes and silver coins.

'You'll be going east the way of my daughter Murdina's?' asked the old woman, watching Barbara counting out the money. 'The Roorahs (Rural Institute) have been learning her how to make scarves on a loom—a little loom that stands on a table. Good day to you, mem.

I'm thanking you for everything, and I'll send
the web to the hotel at Stornoway in Dugald-
the-baker's van. I set the web up on a Thursday
and it was on a Thursday the women came for
the waulking. It's sure to be a lucky web, for
Thursday's the day to begin to weave and
waulk.'

Barbara, feeling as if she were stepping out
of some old 'other world,' made her way to
Murdina's house.

Murdina had been, in her youth, a maid on
the mainland, and had come back to marry
John Macdonald, the crofter at the Crask.
She had a kind heart, an untidy mind, and a
big, young family. The one bright spot in her
life was the Women's Rural Institute meetings,
when the women from all the other townships
gathered round into the little corrugated-iron
hall which was their own property, and where
there was always time for tea and a talk,
besides the pleasure of learning how to do
something new. It's only a tired woman who
knows the pleasure it gives her to sit still and
enjoy tea and home-made scones which someone
else has prepared.

On this particular day Murdina was in a
worse 'steer' than usual. 'Look, you see,
Miss Murray,' she apologized, 'we had the

Communion Season last week, and Angus Macangus, a good and godly man from Harris, was staying with us from the Thursday till the Tuesday, and I was going myself to the church as often as ever I could, and so was my good man, but with Iseaball having the toothache, and the baby not very well, everything got behind.' She produced a scarf. It was of silk and wool, a pretty shade of yellow, with cross-bars of a lighter hue. Murdina had inherited her mother's skill at weaving, but, unfortunately, Johnnie, her small son, had poked a naughty and grimy little hand into the 'sett,' with disastrous results.

'He's that wicked,' his mother mourned. Johnnie, who had the face of an angel and the eyes of an imp, was sitting on a stool, pretending not to hear.

'And when Angus Macangus was taking the Books, he asked Johnnie here didn't he want to be born again, and says Johnnie: "No." And says Angus: "For why not?" And says Johnnie —the little rascal—says he: "In case I might be born a *lassie*."'

Barbara laughed delightedly, and Johnnie, after a quick glance at her face to make sure she was laughing *with* and not *at* him, giggled happily.

'Tis for the winsome lasses too,
Just like my dainty bells of blue.
So weave well the bright threads,
The red threads, the green threads;
Woof well the strong threads
That bind their hearts to mine." '

CHAPTER II

THE EXHIBITION

THE DUCHESS OF NORTHLAND, who had Highland blood in her veins and a warm Highland heart in her breast, had lent her huge house for the Exhibition. That alone ensured an excellent and fashionable class of customers.

There were piles of tweeds, stacks of tartans, forests of socks and golf-stockings, flowergardens of Fair Isle jumpers, and rainbows of scarves, caps and gloves.

Barbara had persuaded a Highland girl who was a nurse in 'Bart's' to dress up like a 'cailleach' and sit by a spinning-wheel. This proved a picturesque and profitable arrangement, and the Highland nurse turned quite a number of 'honest pennies' by allowing daring young ladies to try to spin (at a shilling a trial), and, believe me, spinning is by no means so easy as it looks.

Lady Langcroft (Dorothy Leslie as was) knew to an inch how much tweed was needed for a suit, a swagger coat, a sports skirt or an Inverness cape, and so did her band of assistants.

The Hon. Mrs. Strathoran undertook to run a real Highland tea, with oatcakes, home-made butter and cheese, heather honey and scones, and in order to get the authentic atmosphere she burnt a peat on a soup plate, and used it as a new kind of incense.

Her little daughter Sheena did a roaring trade in buttons and buckles, made out of deer horns, the work of old Farquhar Macleod of Glen Rory, to whom the extra money thus earned would make, for him and his wife, all the difference between bare necessity and comfort.

Barbara had begged Mrs. Mortimer-Smith to *loan* her cat-skin motor-rug to the Exhibition, which so enchanted that lady that she brought it herself, and also brought with her the reluctant and envious Mrs. Ernest Rawson. Barbara made her cup of bliss run over by introducing her to Lady Langcroft, and Mrs. Mortimer-Smith, moved to eloquence, hoped her Ladyship would forgive her for buying the motor-rug, but really she felt she should *die* if she did not get it!

'That would be a great loss,' Lady Langcroft said gently. She had the guileless expression of a turtle dove, and she led Mrs. Mortimer-Smith to certain tweed stalls where were displayed checked materials which up till then had not seemed very popular. Perhaps the checks were rather large in size and loud in hue—blue, red and white predominating.

'These are awfully smart,' said Lady Langcroft, 'but, of course, it is not every woman who can wear them. You need a tall, dignified figure . . . I would look absurd in any of them. . . . But *you* . . .?'

She threw an envious look at Mrs. Mortimer-Smith's well-corseted, buxom figure.

'My sister Molly was clamouring for a sports suit of this red and white, but I simply forbade her! She hasn't the presence *or* the style to carry this check—we both wish we could, for this tweed is quite exclusive. Now, there's this nice quiet brown—it's called "grouse brown" . . .?'

With a lofty sweep of her arm Mrs. Mortimer-Smith brushed aside the nice, quiet 'grouse brown' . . . 'dignity,' 'presence,' 'style,' these were pleasant words, especially when they were applied by a titled lady to an untitled one.

There is no doubt the commercial world has lost a treasure in the way of saleswomanship in Lady Langcroft, who combined with the harmlessness of the dove the wisdom of the serpent. She not only sold a suit length of this

bold check to Mrs. Mortimer-Smith, but
enough of another noisy check to make a
swagger coat, and then as Mrs. Mortimer-
Smith suddenly remembered she was going to
Scotland later on, she invested in a suit length
of the 'grouse brown,' seeing her Ladyship
recommended it.

Lady Langcroft, looking like a bewildered
but pleased child, said in her soft voice, 'And
do go and see Miss Murray's Fair Isle jumpers
—you'll get the very thing you need to wear
with these suits. Please go and tell her I sent
you, and that I shall be very angry with her
if she doesn't find you something nice. By
the way, I don't know that I should either,
when I remember that you took away my
motor-rug! Should I forgive you?' she asked
archly.

Transported with pleasure and pride, Mrs.
Mortimer-Smith, followed by her friend, made
her way to Barbara's stall, and reported what
her Ladyship had said, bought three jumpers,
and only asked the price when she came to
pay for them!

Barbara, quite the affable saleswoman, asked
had Mrs. Mortimer-Smith got what she wanted;
had she seen the tartans? Barbara herself was
wearing a gay Murray tartan skirt, which

looked as if it had been born a kilt and had
grown into a skirt. Her short jacket was the
very next thing to a doublet, and in its lapel
was a sprig of waxen-white bell heather. Yes,
Mrs. Mortimer-Smith rather liked it!

She inquired kindly if Mrs. Mortimer-Smith
had heard of suitable summer quarters, and
was told that quite a long list of possible houses
had been sent to her by Mrs. Macarthur.

'Let me know when you're going north again,
and I'll show you round,' Barbara said con-
fidentially. 'I wish I had time to take you
to the tearoom for a cup of tea, but *do* go and
have some, and ask for oatcakes and heather
honey—they're specially good.' She whispered
mysteriously, 'If you say I sent you, they'll sell
you a section of honey.'

Yes, there was no doubt about it, Mrs.
Mortimer-Smith was having the time of her
life! So were those who served her.

And so was Barbara. The world, she felt,
was so full of a number of things that she, for
one, was very joyous. This joyous feeling had
been bubbling up in her heart ever since the
morning letters had come. One was from
Hugh. He was coming to the Exhibition,
too.

She hadn't seen him for ages (well, for four

months anyway) and there were millions of
things to discuss. Looking back at the past, it
could not be denied that his letters had grown
fewer and shorter. Of course, a congregation
is an exacting taskmaster, she told herself, but
now that the winter's work was over, all that
would be changed.

They had never written love letters to each
other in the accepted term of the words; rather
the letters they exchanged were those of excellent comrades who shared experiences (hadn't
they been in school and in the 'Varsity together?), exchanged thoughts and laughed at
the same jokes.

In one of Barbara's letters to Hugh she had
broached the subject of his taking a charge in
the Highlands. He had evidently been thinking
quite seriously over the matter. 'He's a dear,'
Barbara thought, and planned to write Rebecca
of Applecross, who was a moving spirit on the
Vacancy Committee of the church.

Barbara pictured herself and Hugh happily
settled in a Highland manse. He would help
his people spiritually and materially—he would
write their letters and make their wills and
settle their grievances through the week, and
preach fine helpful sermons on the Sabbath
days. And she . . . oh, she'd try to model

herself on Alison Macarthur, who had made of her manse what a heart is to a body— the core and centre of the parish. She'd keep up her work with the 'Tweeds and Wools.' She knew only too well the difference her coming had made to these crofter homes where money, like Pharaoh's lean kine, is but a vision!

Her second letter was from Andrew Blackwood. He wrote absurd letters, but she enjoyed them. He also was coming to the Exhibition, on condition she didn't make him buy more than one knitted garter, and one woolly glove, his funds being low at the moment. He signed himself happily, 'The Knight of the (One) Garter.' He was a daft laddie in spite of his grave and serious expression, but life was fun, wasn't it?

She was helping Elspeth Craigmyle to make up her mind to buy socks suitable for a friend, and urging her to buy blue ones because 'blue is for love, you know,' when she heard her name called.

A telegraph boy came along shouting, 'Murray—Miss Murray!' Barbara held out her hand. 'I think it's for me,' she said.

It was.

It was from Hugh.

Regret unable to be with you stop explanation follows stop best wishes.   HUGH.

She read it once—she read it twice. 'No bad news, I hope?' queried Elspeth Craigmyle sympathetically.

'No, no, only a friend who was coming can't come,' she replied. 'Now, about golf-stockings? And, by the way, have you seen this bobbin lace? I got a little French lady who is staying in the Highlands to make it for me.'

She went on gaily with her work, and if her heart suddenly felt cold, and dropped like a stone to her heels, no one knew it. There would probably be some excellent explanation—perhaps a funeral, or something which couldn't be put off—in any case 'on with the dance' was the order of the moment. Supposing Andrew Blackwood came, she must have a suitable selection of gloves and garters ready for him to choose from.

But Andrew didn't come. . . . The stalls were cleared, the last customer had gone, the few 'left-overs' were packed away for next time, and the day's takings had been counted and pronounced 'very satisfactory.' The committee were delighted, and made generous acknowledgment of their gratitude to their Organizing Secretary, Miss Barbara Murray.

Barbara 'suitably replied,' as the newspapers say, and departed thankfully to her little flat in Thorburn Gardens.

Hugh's letter was lying on the hall table. She picked it up—threw off her hat—kicked off her shoes—and slumped into her most comfortable chair, and tore open her letter. It wasn't a long letter, but it took a long time to read; there was quite a lot of it 'written between the lines.'

Hugh was disappointed, but Molly Swanson, who had been his right hand in church work all that winter, had trained the Sunday school children for an Operetta. She had asked Hugh to preside, and, of course, Barbara would understand that a minister must put his congregation first; so he had decided to stay and help Molly. The only disappointment was that the dates of the Exhibition and of this Operetta were the same. He was sure Barbara would be glad to hear that the Operetta was likely to be a huge success and the money, after paying some trifling expenses, was to go to various church schemes.

He had been thinking seriously over Barbara's suggestion that he should take a church in the

Highlands, and after talking the matter over with a friend whose advice he valued, he had come to the conclusion that he could really serve the Church better by taking a charge in a city—and there had been a city deputation in his church last Sunday, and they had evidently been favourably impressed. He ended by asking her when was she coming to Abergower, and was 'ever yours, Hugh.'

Barbara laid down the letter, and her face all at once looked old and grey and hopeless.

She smiled bitterly when she recalled that it was *she* who had written Hugh on Molly's behalf . . . Molly was making her a strange return for kindness received!

Presently she'd laugh at the whole business —but not yet—no, not yet. . . . She'd prefer to sit and face the situation. But, oh dear, dear, how cold it was, and how cheerless her flat looked. Why had she not noticed before that the flowers in her vases were withered? And why was her fire smoking? And why didn't her housekeeper bring her tea?

She took up Hugh's letter and read it again, and let the tides of misery sweep over her. She did not hear the door-bell ringing, nor Gladys her housekeeper showing in a visitor. When she raised a pair of miserable eyes, they met the brown, friendly ones of Andrew Black-wood—his white teeth flashing in his lean, brown face, his one wrist bandaged and in his other hand a huge bunch of anemones—in his buttonhole a sprig of white bell heather.

CHAPTER 12

RED FOR COURAGE

She had not seen him since that memorable snowstorm, and although they had exchanged a few letters, she suddenly felt as if this young man who was smiling at her was a stranger—not the same as the writer of the letters at all. It was absurd to feel shy—but she did; there was no blinking the fact. She was even 'blate.' It's a trouble more infectious than the measles, and much quicker at its job, too, for now Andrew was looking shy and embarrassed.

They were a pair of silly asses, she told herself, and made a courageous grab at her usual, cheery, matter-of-fact manner.

'Mr. Blackwood! I'm so glad to see you,' she said and held out her hand. Then she noticed his damaged wrist. 'What have you been doing to yourself?' she inquired. 'Here, take this chair; it's really much more comfortable than it looks. Have you been in another storm?'

He laughed, his eyes dancing with fun. 'A motor one, this time. My car, I call him the "Bluebottle" because he buzzes so much, squared up to a large, respectable limousine, and got snubbed for his pains. His wings and bonnet are gone "phut," and I got a few small damages myself—a cut wrist being one of them. But we saved the dog.'

'The dog?'

'Yes. Didn't I explain that there was a little Scots terrier on the road, and the Bluebottle swerved to avoid the dog, and thus came to conclusions with the aristocratic limousine?'

'I see,' she said thoughtfully. 'I hope your wrist isn't badly hurt?'

He said no, a mere scratch, and added as he had acquired a dog, it was really 'A Good Thing'; he had always wanted a dog of his own, and he had bought this one from its owner, who complained that London was no place for a dog.

Just to avoid an embarrassing silence, Barbara began a spirited description of the motor-car *she* had acquired, the gift of a member of the committee who had no further use for it.

'Oh, thank you so much for these lovely flowers. Please excuse me while I put them into water.'

The fire suddenly ceased sulking, and sprang into a cheerful blaze. With a bowl of glorious anemones on the table, and the cheerful tinkle

if I had known I would not have written my friends in the Highlands and suggested your name to them. They were so pathetically pleased, poor dears! It's going to be rather ghastly to write and tell them of your decision. Because they are living in an out-of-the-world part of Scotland instead of in one of its cities, it is foolish of them to expect a first-class preacher.

'I seem to remember that the Master was quite pleased to preach a most wonderful sermon to a congregation of one, and that a woman—a Samaritan sinner. When she spoke of the Messiah whom they all expected, He told her what He had never told the Jews. He said: "I that speak unto thee am He."

'Samaria would have missed quite a lot if He had elected to go with His disciples to the city instead of sitting by the well of Jacob.

'No, I do not expect to be in Abergower for quite a long while. I am sorry you are still so busy that you can spare only a few minutes to write me. (I am quoting your own words.) Please don't bother doing so any more.

'BARBARA.'

Lest she should change her mind, she rushed forth and posted this letter in the pillar-box at the end of the Gardens, and then came in and wept bitterly, for she had said good-bye, not only to Hugh, but to dear and lovely dreams. She was facing loneliness. No one needed her. She was a superfluous woman.

As she lay wide awake in bed, words she had heard on her wanderings suddenly said themselves over and over in her brain. They were: 'Blue for love, green for youth, and red for courage.'

Youth and love had passed her by. Her next birthday would be her thirtieth. There was nothing of her youth left; she must take red for courage, and weave it bravely into her web of life.

CHAPTER 13

BLUE FOR LOVE

SUMMER had come to the Highlands, a summer of singing burns and balmy airs. Patches of snow still lingered on the tops of the bens, but the glens were clothed with loveliest green, and already the bell heather made splashes of royal crimson on the hillsides, and the pines and fir trees looked as if they were climbing up and up the mountain-side, their slogan being 'Excelsior.' From remote distances came the cry of the curlew, and the 'go-back, go-back' of the grouse. Already the young birds were strong on the wing and lusty in the voice, happily unconscious of the twelfth of August.

Barbara, pounding along in Phœbe, stopped to gather a bunch of bog myrtle and bell heather. This kind of heather always made her think of Shenag, and by quick transition of thought her mind went back to Andrew Blackwood and their experience in the snow-storm.

Looking back at the past months, she had to admit she had been seeing quite a lot of

Andrew, especially since that April day of the Exhibition—a day that was indeed an April one!

Andrew's presence that miserable evening had helped her wonderfully. He was often in London; his work, he explained carefully, made it necessary to visit the London labs.; Manchester and London must each know what the other was doing. He had always time to come to see her, too, to take her out to dinner and a show; to listen with interest to all she had to tell him about her work; to laugh with her over her latest joke, and to sympathize with her when her plans miscarried, as they sometimes did. Oh, they were excellent friends — nothing more . . . she often said so.

Once he had asked her might he write an urgent letter in her flat. She said, 'Yes, of course,' and cleared her desk, and gave him her own writing materials.

While he wrote, she sat down by the fireside and took up a piece of knitting she was doing in her spare moments. He had brought with him on this occasion the Scottie that he had rescued—an adorable dog with a trusty face, wise eyes, and an engaging way of sitting upon the feet of those he liked. His name was

Hector, and he wore a tartan collar with a Tailwaggers' medal on it.

Barbara and he were fast friends; he didn't admit all and sundry into his heart, but those he did were there 'for keeps.'

'Move off my ball, please, Hector,' Barbara said in a whisper.

She did not wish to disturb the man busy with his urgent letter. She stole a look at his intent face . . . and at that very moment he looked up—their eyes met. A look passed between them then that was to both of them an unforgettable thing.

'How do you spell Portuguese?' he asked.

She told him. He smiled his thanks—his eyes lingering on the picture she made sitting there in her fireside chair, her knitting in her hands and the dog sprawling on her feet.

'Spell it again. I didn't quite catch what you said.'

'Pay attention,' she said sternly; but the smile which accompanied her words wasn't stern. No.

He turned back to his writing. Perhaps his head and his heart were registering such exciting emotions he had no time to notice what he was doing with his hands, but at any rate he managed to upset the ink bottle.

'Oh, look what I've done! I *am* an awkward brute.'

Barbara flew to his rescue. 'Never mind the desk, I'll mop up the ink with blotting paper; but look at your sleeve! It's soaked! Off with your jacket at once. Gladys is awfully good at taking out stains.'

He was still upbraiding himself, and trying to tidy up the mess, when she returned.

'We think we've got out the ink stains,' she said, 'but you must wait for a few minutes till the sleeve dries, and, by the way'—she made a sudden dive for her knitting—'stand straight up, will you? I want to see if this is long enough.'

She held her knitting against his chest— oh, in the most matter-of-fact fashion (though her hands trembled a little)—she frowned as she examined what was evidently a pullover in the making.

'Scarcely long enough,' she mused, giving it a tug. 'Rather wide, too.' Then, looking up with a bright smile, she asked, 'Why are you so thin?'

'I've always been thin,' he said, as if this were a good reason! 'When my mother was living she used to make me drink bottles of cod-liver oil. After she died no one bothered;

but, I say . . .' His voice was suddenly shy
and warm, 'Do you mean you're knitting this
—this thing——'

'Pullover,' she corrected.

'Pullover, then—for me?'

'Such is indeed my intention'; she was
doing mysterious things with an inch tape and
a paper of safety-pins. Hector regarded them
with indulgent eyes.

'You see,' she went on chattily (bother those
shaky hands of hers), 'I happened to notice
that this wool was an exact match for your
suit—it was asking to be knitted into a pullover.
Would you mind standing still for a moment?
Yes, that's better; your waist, like the Equator,
is an imaginary line. Well, I had got a new
pattern for a pullover, and I was anxious to
try it out—so this is by way of being an ex-
periment.'

Could anything be more brutally matter-of-
fact? The pity was she couldn't make her
voice sound as brutal as her words.

'Nobody ever knitted things for me since
my mother died. I buy them out of shops—
machine-made, I expect.'

'Quite a satisfactory plan,' she nodded,
'they generally fit better.' She hoped her
words would rouse him to anger; nothing like

good, honest wrath for chasing away sentimental nonsense!

And her words did.

'Home-knitted things are *always* better, even
if they don't fit,' he cried. 'The person who
made them must of necessity have put something of herself into the work, and that's what
no machine can do—that's what makes home-
knitted things so—so—precious.'

She suddenly looked up; he was looking
down. There was a mischievous twinkle in her
eyes, and his were not holden. . . . His arms
were round her, his lips on her hair. 'You
wretch,' he whispered, 'you provoking little
wretch.'

Strange words, but uttered as he uttered
them they sounded like sweetest music. But
only for a split second—next minute she had
withdrawn herself.

Gladys entering with his jacket brought
matters back to an everyday atmosphere again,
but the memory abode with them both. Such
things are not easily forgotten, and their re-
membrance is apt to bring with it a feeling
of embarrassment. 'Why,' she asked herself
tragically, 'why can't a man and a woman be
friends—just friends?'

It's an old and, as yet, unanswered question.

She was still asking herself this question as she sped along the road on this glorious summer morning. She told herself that she had found her life's work in 'Wools and Tweeds.' Could any woman wish for a happier or a more useful life? 'Count your blessings, Barbara,' she admonished herself. 'If there is no husband and home for you in the future, just think how many homes your work has helped. You're inclined to be a sentimental ass, my girl.'

A motor-lorry was drawn up at the side of the road, and the driver was plunging head-long into its 'innards.' The lorry was loaded mountains high with sacks of wood.

'Anything wrong?' Barbara asked.

The driver—he was a little thin wisp of a man with a pair of bright blue eyes and a face like a wrinkled, winter apple—emerged from the engine, and gave her a bright smile.

'One of the plugs is dirty,' he announced. 'Aye, it's a little thing, but because it's clogged wi' ile and dirt, it's hinderin' a' the rest o' the machinery.' He struggled manfully with a spanner and an oily rag, then he used the rag to wipe his brow, which was streaming with sweat.

He looked at his work. 'Aye, that's better,' he said.

The indomitable pluck of the little man, who was obviously old and weary, touched Barbara's heart.

'Isn't that lorry too heavy for you?' she asked.

'Not a bit,' he answered cheerily. 'I'm stronger the day than I was a twelvemonth ago. Then I was doin' nothing, except potterin' aboot the hoose and the gairden. I used tae work in the quarry up yonder, but when it was closed doon I was peyed off—so were a' the ithers. I'd a bittie money saved and lyin' in the bank, and a few pounds ma brither Donald from America left me. I had nothing to complain aboot, like the men wi' wives and bairns. They had to go on the dole —aye, that's a meeserable business, noo.'

Barbara unearthed from her car a bag of bananas, and asked her fellow-traveller to have one, which he did thankfully, leaning against the lorry while he ate it.

'Well, one day I heard that the Quarry Wud was for sale, an' I began tae think. Supposin' I bocht the standin' wud—got men tae cut doon the trees—sold the trunks tae the joiners in the toon—for their work—chopped up the branches into firewood—would it nae gi'e work tae twa-three idle men? I thocht

127

aboot it, an' I asked the Lord tae guide me, an'
He said, "Launch out into the deep, and let
down your net for a draught." An' I did. It
meant I had tae tak' ma bawbees oot o' the
bank — buy a second-hand motor-lorry — buy
the Quarry Wud, an' engage as many men as
I could affoord.'

He paused, his eyes bright at some pleasant
thought. 'Foo mony men, think ye, ha'e I?'

'Ten,' she guessed.

'No, but—*seventeen*!' He gave a crow of
triumphant laughter. 'Seventeen,' he repeated,
'an' that means that every Setterday nicht I
pey seventeen men their wages, an' their wives
can buy their Sunday beef, an' ken the money
is *earned*—it's no' dole.'

'Well done,' Barbara congratulated him.
'It warms my heart to hear things like this.'

'I wasna sure, mind you, just at first foo the
thing was tae work oot—but I'd faith in God.
He put the notion in ma heid, an' He has helped
me—the business is peyin' fine. I ha'e steady
customers in a' the toons roond aboot, an' at
the Quarry Wud there's nae unemployment.'
He turned the words over in his mouth as if
he liked the sound of them. 'Noo, mem, I must
be off—thank ye kindly for the bananas, oh,
thank ye—are ye meanin' me tae tak' the hale

bag o' them? Weel-a-weel, I'm awful obleeged —there's naething I like better nor a ripe banana—they're that easy tae eat if ye've nae teeth, an' I've only twa left, but still I should be thankful—they're opposite ane anither.'

His brave story told so simply touched her heart. She had been grumbling about her life; he was an old hero of seventy, launching out into the unknown deep when he might quite justifiably stay in the harbour. He was letting down his net, and by so doing was helping seventeen homes. The world seemed a better, happier place because of the story she had just heard. Yet there are croakers among us who insist upon it that the world is growing steadily worse.

Nannie Sinclair's door was open. This was such a strange sight, she paused to look and wonder, for Nannie was 'a'body's body,' and was so much in request she was hardly ever at home. If there was a sick person to nurse— a sleepless baby to coax into sleep—a weary woman to help with her washing—you'd find Nannie there; it was even reported that little Tom Alick Sutherland proposed changing his own mother for Nannie—but this, of course, may be mere idle scandal.

I

'How are you to-day, Nannie?' Barbara asked, stepping indoors.

Nannie was on her knees on the floor, a worried expression on her face, and a piece of blue pipeclay in her hand.

She had been sketching a pattern upon what was to be a '*clootie bass*'—in other words, a rag hearthrug—and finding it difficult to get her hand to obey her head.

She explained to Barbara that the borders of the rug were not so bad, but she had set her heart upon having in the middle of the rug the words, 'Home, Sweet Home,' and, 'It's as sure as you're there, I canna get the "S" tae look richt.'

Barbara examined the letter. 'You're turning it the wrong way,' she said gently. 'Do you mind if I change it?'

Nannie watched with breathless gratitude.

'There's an "S" on the weathercock on the schoolhouse, an' it was there I was lookin',' she explained artlessly. 'But yon "S" is ootside-in, I'm thinkin'.'

Barbara chuckled. 'Would you like me to sketch all the words?' she asked.

'It's masel' that would,' Nannie cried.

'I'll take my fountain pen, then. The ink in it won't rub out so easily as pipeclay. This is to be a very "posh" rug,' she went on chattily.

Nannie, crouching on a 'creepie' stool, her hands clasped on her knees, watched with great interest the magic of Barbara's penmanship. 'There's yonder on the *Highland Sentinel* an "S" wi' a curly-wurly thingumbob on its head—awful bonny,' she hinted.

'Show me the *Highland Sentinel*,' cried Barbara.

Nannie showed her the paper and immediately the 'S' on the rug was adorned with 'curly-wurly thingumbobs.'

'I might do the same with the "H's,"' she said, proud ambition having now got possession of her.

Nannie beamed.

'That's beautiful,' she said. 'It's for Marget Budge's birthday—Marget and her man are going for a holiday, an' I'm tae look efter the hoose an' bairns till they come back.'

This was startling news; to go for a holiday in the Highlands is considered quite as silly as, and much more expensive than, to go for a walk.

'Ye see, Peter Budge has been ill,' Nannie went on. 'He's farm manager doon at Craig-Sheen, an' didn't he fall doon the ootside stairs o' the granary an' break his leg. Well-a-well,

Doctor Broon came at once, an' says he, "We'll
take Peter tae the hospital," but Peter says,
"You'll do no such thing. You'll take me
home to Marget, an' she'll nurse me." Doctor
Broon thinks for a meenit, then says he, "All
right—I'll go first and tell your wife. She'll
get a fright when she sees the ambulance
coming," an' when they reached Peter's hoose
(an' they took a long time, for at every step
Peter would bawl oot o' him) they found that
the doctor had, with his own hands, taken doon
Peter's bed from the upstairs room and set it
up in the kitchen. Are you putting a curly
thing on the last letter? Oh, that's just an
ornament, is it? Well-a-well, Peter was *that*
annoyed when he saw this, that he says, "You'll
carry me up the stair." "We'll do no such
thing," says the doctor; "you'll be an awful
bother to your wife as it is, but if you were
in bed up the stair you'd be a bigger bother."
Peter never thocht he was any bother, an' the
doctor's words angered him. "Marget's no
one tae hain her steps," says he, an' says
the doctor, "Don't I know that. Look at the
thinness of her, and her hair is grey and her
face is pale—and I can mind what a bonny,
rosy lass she was when she married you,
Peter Budge." He said more—he said some-

thing aboot Marget every time he came. He asked Peter tae look at her tired face—"And can you expect her no' tae look tired an' her sleeping on a shakedown beside you, an' rising at six o'clock to get the boys off tae their work, an' the little ones tae school?" Peter saw for the first time in his life what a weary life a woman body leads, an' how her work is never done, an' by the time he was able to put his leg below him, he was a changed man. It was the doctor's doings! Myself was going west to help Marget, an' then the doctor said, "What about a holiday? Nannie here will look after everything till you come back," and Peter says, "All right, doctor." Would you think I should put a puckle o' red thread in the inside border?'

Barbara said, 'Yes. Go on about Peter and Marget, you haven't told me why you're making the *clootie bass*.'

Nannie chuckled. 'That was another thing Peter noticed when he was lying in the kitchen bed—the bass that was before the fire was in holes, and every time Marget walked over it her feet were catching in it, and she'd no time tae mend it. He spoke aboot it tae me on the quiet, and says I, "Wouldn't it be a good thing tae give Marget a new one?" and he was awful pleased, and asked would I make it.

He's no' a bad man, poor Peter, it's just that he doesna think; and so we planned the *clootie bass*, and then he minded that her birthday was on the twentieth of this month, and I'm trying tae get it ready, with "Home, Sweet Home" in the middle of it.'

How much of this arrangement was due to Nannie's kind and understanding heart one need not ask, but never did a homely *clootie bass* stand for more.

'I have a bunch of blue wool in my car,' Barbara said, 'you might use it for the "Home, Sweet Home."'

'An' thank you kindly, my dear, I will,' said Nannie, 'blue, you know, is for love, an' it's love that makes all agree.'

CHAPTER 14

GREEN FOR YOUTH

In the little hall at Achmore, Barbara met a crowd of her cailleachs, each with something to sell, and something to tell too of how she had managed it.

It was amazing how much originality some of her workers showed, especially in the knitting of jumpers, pullovers and golf-stockings. Coarse wool had been woven into mats upon which it would seem heaven-daring to set one's feet! It was clear from the multitude of colours that there had been some daring experiments with dyeing; Barbara was always specially interested in this branch of her work.

It was touching, too, to listen to the women's plans for spending the money they thus earned. New shoes for little Hughie, a new winter coat for Janet, a Sabbath-day hat for 'the man,' meaning the husband and father of the home. 'It's as sure as you're there, Hector hasn't got a new hat since we were married, and that's five-and-twenty years ago. It's quite good yet, of course, for he only wears it at funerals, and communion times, and occasions, but didn't the mice chow a hole in the crown of it, and we never knew till himsel' was going west to Colin Stewart's funeral.'

Eppie Scott, a born humorist, had an engaging tale to tell of how she was to spend part of her money.

'An *umberella*,' she said solemnly, 'as beeg an umberella as I can get.'

It seemed a useful thing to buy, Barbara thought.

'You see, mem,' Eppie went on, 'Adam, my man, bought a shelt an' a spring cairt at old Mrs. Strathbeg's roup. The shelt seemed a nice, quate beastie, an' the cairt was light and handy. She used to go to the church in it, but she was a delicate craitur, an' suffered awful wiss neuterology in the heid; so when she was going to the church she always kept her umberella open—it was a big one an' had belonged to him that's gone—her husband, I mean. Adam was thinking that we might be going west to the church in the spring cairt, too, but it's as sure as you're there, when the shelt saw him in his Sabbath-day clothes, he wouldn't stir a step! He just put his four feet down on the ground—an' out o' that *he-would-not-stir*! We tried him wiss a handful o' sugar—a carrot—an' an aipple—an' then a good hard stick. It was for no use. He wouldn't budge.

'Old Hamish from the hill was passing to the church at the time, and says he to Adam, "Try the shelt wiss your umberella, Adam."

'"What's wrong wiss a whip?" says he.

'"Oh, not to whip him," says Hamish, "but to show him. Stop you—I know the ways o' the beastie."

'Hamish climbed up into the cairt, an' opened the old ancient umberella he always carried on the Sabbath day, an' the shelt took one *keek* over his shoulder—sees the umberella —an' *bolted*! He went as quick as one o' this telegrams—as sure as you're there! Hamish brought him back covered wiss sweat, an' says he, "That's how to make him go, Adam—the whip is no use, only the open umberella"—so now, that's why I'm going to the town to buy a big one.' Eppie's eyes twinkled roguishly. It was a good story, and lost nothing in the telling, and Barbara proved a most sympathetic listener.

She also suggested a gaily striped golf umbrella, but it seemed the shelt (a creature of strong likes and dislikes) preferred the green-but-once-black variety, and till such time as this aid-to-progress was bought, Eppie's family had either to walk to church or stay at home.

It was a pleasant thought to Barbara that the money she was able to distribute was bringing so much happiness and comfort. She told herself so several times over—she told herself she was a lucky woman to have a job so rich in human interest. Then, inconsistent as every woman is, she sighed impatiently, and wondered what letters would be waiting her when she got back to her lodgings that evening.

All these women with whom she had been having dealings had husbands, or brothers, or bairns, to whom her coming meant such a lot; she herself was a lonely old spinster—old, yes, very old—she felt about ninety as she wended her way to her temporary home.

She wanted a home that 'stayed put'; as it was, she was like a wayfaring man who turns aside for a night and resumes his journey next morning. That was enough to make any woman feel old.

Mrs. Maclure, the shepherd's wife with whom she lodged, had baked for her supper a noble gingerbread cake—there were ham and eggs, too, and oatcakes, and because Whity the cow had calved there was plenty of milk and cream and butter. So life wasn't so dreary after all!

Letters? Oh yes, John-the-post left a number

—Mrs Maclure had laid them all out on the mantelpiece. 'And if you please, mem, will I just be confusing the tea?'

Barbara said, 'Yes, please,' and hurried to examine the letters. She always got so many of these, one would think she might not be excited, but she was. She carried in her heart the incurable belief that some day a letter was to reach her which would change her life. It was strange that on this summer evening in the shepherd's little cosy house such a letter did reach her. Sometimes one's dreams do come true!

And after she had read it, years and years dropped from her shoulders; green youth shone out of her eyes; dimples played hide-and-seek round her mouth. Better, far better, than any mere cosmetic was the letter brought to her by John-the-post.

Oblivious of the time—and of her scarcely touched supper—she dreamed on. 'I'll sleep over it, and write an answer to-morrow,' she told herself. But when she went to bed, sleep eluded her. She lay wide awake, planning a suitable reply to this disturbing but delightful letter. Daylight was creeping over the land ere she did at last fall asleep.

CHAPTER 15

AGAIN WE ROB THE POST-BAG

'THE SHIELING,
'*July* 22, 19—.

'*To* Sir Andrew Blackwood,
    'Knight of the Garter (*a*) one, (*b*) woolly.

'DEAR SIR KNIGHT,
    'Your very welcome letter, along with a few not
so welcome, and one Most Important, were waiting
me when I returned to my temporary quarters in
The Shieling.
    'By the way, one of the not-so-welcome letters was
from a customer who had ordered golf-stockings for
her husband, and the said stockings turn out to be
too big. What do I propose to do about it? she
asks. . . . I'm sure I don't know.
    'It was the sort of letter to which I should have
grown accustomed, though I never do; bad-tempered
handwriting, spelling somewhat "wonky," and beginning in the third person, her feelings had evidently got too much for her and she ended up in the
first with a regular shower of marks, exclamations
and interrogations. She wants her money back, too,
unless I can suggest a remedy for the hose. I'd like
to tell her to boil the stockings, like Shirley Temple's
kilt, till she got them a right size. But I dare not
write in this frivolous strain. A horrid person! I
shall answer her to-morrow in my best commercial
style.
    'And now to the letter marked Most Important.
It's from Mr. Mortimer-Smith (by the way, it turns

out his name is James). Did I, in a hasty moment, say he reminded me of a surprised rabbit or an astonished robin? If so, I apologize—I grovel!

'Really, I'm so excited, that it's impossible to be even faintly coherent. Wait, please, till I refill my fountain pen, get a fresh sheet of notepaper, and a grip of my grammar.

'*Later.*

'I'm slightly calmer now, thank you. Where was I? Oh yes. Mr. Mortimer-Smith, whom I considered a negligible quantity, turns out to be quite a big noise in the world of wool. He has mills in the Midlands, and is the chief partner in a company called Hallifields—do you know it?

'He has something to do with wool in New Zealand and Australia, and (am I boring you?—never mind —the thrill is about due) his manager in South Island, who is a Scotsman, wants a competent woman to be sent out to New Zealand to begin a "Tweed and Wool" business there, the same as I've been doing in this country. . . . And Mr. Mortimer-Smith, it now appears, was very much impressed by my business capabilities, both on meeting me in the Manse when I sold his wife a motor-rug, and also by the reports brought home by that lady as well as the goods from our Exhibition. . . . And now he asks me *will I take on the job*! The salary offered is so huge I think it must be a joke. Now then. How's that for a thrill? Have you recovered your breath, for I have scarcely done so?

'I'm to try to compose a suitable reply, but I thought I'd like to tell someone of my amazing good fortune first. And you see, I'm like yourself, rather a lonely person; my brother Bob is, of course, interested, but he has a wife and bairns, and they naturally come first, and I'm quite out of maiden aunts and cousins!

'I think I could get Morag Macleod, who at the moment is a nurse in Bart's, to undertake my work —I'd train her for a month before departing. By the way, did I tell you they want me in the autumn, or early in the winter?

'It's a humiliating but wholesome truth that none of us are indispensable; my first thought was that *I* was, but second and more sensible thoughts tell me I'm nothing of the kind. Morag would do very well—in fact, better than I, for she can speak Gaelic.

'Phœbe is still behaving like a perfect lady, and she and I are going to see my dear friends at the Kyle to-morrow, and then on to Shenag Macleod and her mother. I must wangle that dye formula out of them this time, or perish—and you wouldn't like me to perish, would you? No, no, besides I'm going to New Zealand, a new and wonderful adventure. True, I have occasional qualms about it, but they are only occasional—the rest of the time I'm simply bursting with sinful pride. . . . I'm not allowing myself to think of how homesick I may be. Bother Scotland! What right has she to bespell her bairns when they want to fare forth in search of high adventures. Write to me, and tell me you're pleased.

'   Ever yours sincerely,
'   BARBARA MURRAY.'

'THE SHIELING,
'*July* 22, 19—.

' *To* Mrs. Alison Macarthur,
'   The Manse.
'AILIE, MY DEAR,

'Wind, weather and Phœbe all being agreeable, I'm hoping to look in at the Manse to-morrow

142

evening. I've heaps of things to tell you. You know, of course, that once upon a time I was rather looking forward to being a minister's wife myself. But of course that was absurd. The minister concerned agreed when I said so, and for quite a month I thought my heart was broken. It wasn't. But my pride was hurt most horribly—I'm better now, thank you.

'You know, Ailie, I've been giving my mighty mind to the subject of ministers' wives. There are two classes of them. One is the *Shining Example*, like you, and the other is the *Awful Warning*, like I'd be. So seeing I'm spared this trying experience, and seeing the minister is also spared it, poor lamb, instead of being a very bad minister's wife and an Awful Warning, I'm going forth to New Zealand to start a "Tweed and Wool" campaign on the same lines as I'm working here in Scotland. Isn't life amusing? I think Fate must have a strong sense of humour, and why not?

'You'll never guess who has put this high adventure my way? Mrs. Mortimer-Smith . . .! And to think I suggested to you that you should send her looking for summer quarters to houses that had steep and damp footpaths, and cracked kitchen ranges. She came, you remember, accompanied by her husband, and I so impressed the little man that he has offered me this job. But I must not forget that it's all through his wife.

'I heard a new and delightful word yesterday— one of my cailleachs, resenting the coming of a stranger to the district, said, "And what are we wanting an *anteloper* for?" Isn't it a delightful word? Well, I'm to be an *anteloper* in New Zealand. I see an opening there for a wicked pun, but I won't take it. No.

'Please do try to keep an hour free for me; tell the congregation you can't be bothered with them, though I really can't imagine you ever saying that, Ailie, my dear. In any case, keep a little while for your highly excited old friend,

'BABS.'

CHAPTER 16

THE DYE AT LAST

THE moor, which had looked so desolate that winter afternoon in the snowstorm, was now a royal glory of purple bell heather when Barbara visited it in the end of July. Bog cotton waved fairy hands to her—bees plundered the flowers and filled the air with the smell of honey—foxgloves, like tall flames, stood up here and there—the blue sky bent over all, and the little burn wandered onward to the sea, singing as it went. In the distance the hills stood, their feet in the moor, their heads in the clouds. The air quivered. The beauty of the earth was so gripping it gave her pleasure that was almost pain.

She wondered how she'd feel about it all when she was in New Zealand, and thousands of miles separated her from the land of her birth. But this was nonsense. Meantime she must drink her fill of the beauty and the spaciousness of the world.

She drew Phœbe to the side of the road and, armed with an ancient sunshade which she used as a walking-stick, she set forth on a little voyage of exploration. The railway helped to guide her so far—but where was the bothy where she had bathed her blistered heel— where she had spent a queer but nice hour with another storm-stayed wedding-guest—and where she had met that rather alarming creature, Shenag Macleod?

Barbara always declared that instead of a bump of locality her head showed a hollow; perhaps that was the reason she took a totally wrong direction in searching for the bothy. But she didn't mind.

The warmth of the air, the hum of the bees, always a companionable cheery sound, so enraptured her she burst into song.

Now, no one—not even those who loved her —could say Barbara was a good singer. But mercifully there was no other human being within sight or sound, so it didn't matter.

On and on she wandered—the winding sheep tracks so intrigued her she just had to see where they led to. She must have wandered for miles—she was quite out of sight of the road by this time—when suddenly she stopped singing. There was another sound, a sinister, terrible one, which shattered the silence as glass is shattered by a fall. A wild scream—

another—and then an ugly sound like a wild beast snarling.

Where were the sounds coming from?

Unused to the space of the moor, she found it difficult to locate the sounds. She stood on a braeside, gazing anxiously and at first in the wrong direction. Then came a muffled scream nearer—in fact, quite near her. A free fight seemed to be going on in a little hollow. From where she stood Barbara could neither distinguish number nor sex, but that cry had sounded like a woman's voice, and it was a cry for help.

She tucked her skirt well over her knees and rushed to the rescue. She lost her beret on the way and a rash step sent her headlong into a peaty pool, from which she emerged considerably the worse and mud from head to heels, but she couldn't wait to wash the mud off her face, for again that cry for help sounded. Clutching her sunshade (its cover had come undone and was hanging in strips) she tore on.

So fierce was the fight the combatants did not notice her till she was close to them. Two boys were struggling with a frenzied woman, and quite literally tooth and nail were being used, and the air was thick with Gaelic curses —no language to touch it for these!

'You bullying brutes, let go,' Barbara panted,

and rained a shower of blows on the boys' heads. 'You—dirty—little—cads,' she said, punctuating each word with a blow. 'Take that—and that—and that.' She paused at last, not for want of will, but for want of breath, also the stick of her sunshade was broken.

One of the boys turned on her; but Barbara had not been one of the best hockey players in her school for nothing. She caught the boy by the shoulders, shook him, and turned him upside down. The other boy, seeing his companion so thoroughly handled, fled incontinently. When Barbara raised her eyes, she met the dancing and astonished ones of a man who had come to the rescue, but from a different direction.

Her face was deadly white, except where it was black with mud, her eyes were blazing, her hair was tousled, and her collar had come undone. Yet Andrew Blackwood thought he had never seen her looking so bonny!

She was far too angry to be astonished at anything. Her capacity for wonder was gone.

'The two of them—set on this poor creature,' she said, and then she turned to look at the woman for whom she had fought. '*Shenag!*' she cried, 'why, Shenag, what *is* the meaning of this?'

Shenag, a pitiable-looking creature, with the tears running down her bruised and bleeding face, sobbed out an explanation. She had been looking for white bell heather, and the boys, who were always after her, had set on her and tried to take it from her.

'Just let me get my hands on them,' Barbara flashed. But the boys had gone! They stayed not on the order of their going, either.

'They seem to have been in rather a hurry,' Andrew said, with a smile. But Barbara was in no mood for frivolity. Instead she looked at Shenag and said, 'We'll take you home.' She patted the poor creature tenderly. 'Come along,' she said, and led the way.

'If I might mention it, you're going in the wrong direction,' Andrew said meekly.

Then they both laughed.

Barbara's capacity for losing herself was an old joke between them; somehow the memory of it helped to bring this strange meeting into a more everyday atmosphere.

'But why are you here?' she asked suddenly.

'May I not take a stroll over the moor if I have a mind to? Of course, I did not charge along in the headlong fashion you did, neither did I arm myself with a sunshade or tumble into a muddy pool—I believe the technical

name is "a peat hag." I have too much respect
for my clothes—especially *this*,' he patted his
pullover, and she saw with a thrill of pleasure
it was the one she had knitted for him.

Suddenly she was painfully conscious of her
untidy appearance.

'Lead on, Macduff,' she said, trying to speak
jauntily. 'I'll follow when I do something
about my—my—sleeve.'

'Sleeve, did you say, or skirt?'

She stole a hurried glance at this garment,
and what she saw made her blush rosy red.
He left her to it, for which she was thankful.
It was too bad that her stockings as well as
her skirt should have played her false. They
had developed veritable Jacob's ladders.

Shenag's mother was standing in the door.
She hobbled painfully to meet them, and
Shenag in a flood of passionate Gaelic told
what had happened, and how the kind leddy
who had once given her a bonny scarf had
rescued her from the boys who tried to rob her.

Her mother listened with blazing eyes.
Then she clenched her old hands, and raising
them above her head she called down maledictions on the black hearts and evil hands of
those who had tried to rob her lassie.

'If I had the money, it's back to the Lews I would be going, where the people are kind and where I can get the right kind of fish for my dye,' she said in English, and then turning to Andrew and Barbara she cried, as one invoking a blessing, 'And may the Benign Being bless you both and make you happy. May you never want a friend to help you, a roof to cover you, a fire to warm you or love to fill your hearts.'

She turned and limped into the house, and when she came back she was carrying a small parcel wrapped in oil silk.

'It's the secret of the dye,' she whispered, pressing it into Barbara's hands. 'You deserve it—you and your husband. It will be doing good to you, for, look see, since I came here I could never get the fish that makes the purple dye. I had to use the "madder," and that isn't so good.'

Then she led Shenag into the house, saying as they went, 'Be coming in, *m'eudail*, and your old mother will be putting a salve on your hurts.'

Mother and daughter disappeared into the house. Andrew and Barbara stood still, exchanging puzzled looks, Barbara still holding the little packet which smelled strongly of peat reek.

Then Andrew had a brain wave—at least, so he said. 'Let's go to the roadman's bothy. You remember it? We can rest in it for a few minutes, and try to sort out things. I have biscuits. Abernethy ones. Perhaps when we find the kettle and a basin of water——?'

'I haven't a blistered heel this time.'

'N-n-no,' he admitted.

'I suppose my face is dirty. I left my bag in Phœbe. I might do something about my face if I had it.'

'I'll fetch it,' he volunteered. 'I left the Bluebottle parked beside your car. By the way, you forgot to turn off your engine.'

Annoying! She frowned and tried to carry it off with a high hand. 'I didn't mean to be away for more than five minutes.' She implied that for such a short time there was no need to bother.

'Here's the bothy; let's rest for a bit. Yes, I turned off the engine. But first I drew your car nearer the edge of the road. After all, the road is narrow, and there might be other passers-by. Hullo, the door is open!' He looked in.

Suddenly he sprang from her side, and made a dive at something growing behind the sunless back of the bothy.

152

'Allow me to present to you a bunch of white bell heather,' he said, bowing low, and holding out a regular clump of lovely waxen flowers. 'And the hand which holds it goes with the heather.'

For a man who imagined he was 'blate,' Andrew managed this little ceremony very nicely. And Barbara?

Her face registered every emotion from A to Z, then with eyes dancing with fun she said, 'Who but me would have a proposal of marriage when her face isn't even clean—when her skirt is hanging in ribbons round her laddered stockings? Oh, Andrew!' She held out her hand for the heather.

Next minute his arms were round her—her words were choked out against his shoulder . . . the smell of his Harris tweed coat seemed to stifle her. His lips were warm against her ear, murmuring tenderly, 'My love is like a red, red rose.' He commanded her to lift her eyes to his, and he said—oh, never mind what he said—what he did was more important.

'This is an amazing day,' Barbara said, sometime after; she was the first to recapture her sanity, and then she heard of how her letter telling of her going to New Zealand had sent Andrew flying northward.

'I suppose you think you're the only person who knows Jimmy Smith,' he said, 'but I know him too, and a better little chap never stepped, though his wife, Mrs. Mortimer-Smith, is a bit overpowering. Jimmy is sending me (complete with wife) to New Zealand to look after the man's part of the enterprise. I say, Babs, we'll take the secret dye with us. Let's have a look at the packet! We'll give the old woman a lump sum of money for it, or, if she'd rather, a commission on the sales.'

'Joyful,' Barbara cried. 'Then they can go back to the Lews. I think they'll be happier there. Can't we sit down, Andrew, my legs are groggy.'

'The Abernethy biscuit is called for,' he said, rummaging in his pockets.

'No, it's not,' she laughed. 'Do be sensible, Andrew.'

'I can't be sensible without your help, Babs. I need you.' He turned and looked at her, smiling. 'Barbara,' he said softly, 'I need you —oh, I need you badly.'

She laughed, but her voice was shaky. Andrew had used the one reason which for her was unanswerable. He needed her; to one human being she was indispensable. Her heart voiced a great *Laus Deo*.

'I'm tired to death of loneliness,' he confessed.

'So am I,' she nodded.

She was half-frightened when she saw the look on his face; it was one of exultation. 'God help me to keep green and fragrant the awe and ecstasy of this wonderful moment.'

And here by rights my story should end. But it doesn't! I'm ashamed to confess that Barbara and her Andrew have got the better of me, and just do what they like. . . . Still, I'd like to tell how the dye, the search for which brought them together, and in the end joined them in marriage, proved to be for everyone's material prosperity.

The formula, so carefully cherished by Shenag's mother, told of a certain kind of fish which produced the wonderful blue—a secret shared by the Norsemen and the Irish —the latter, indeed, using it to produce 'Madonna blue.' The plants were bent, which gave red, madder yielded blue and purple, crottle, yellow and brown, goats' hair and wool mixed gave black and white, green came from the heather, and in order to make the dyes fast each had its own hour of gathering — each its own hour of brewing — and each its own spell of incantation. . . . Witches had been known to steal the dye out of the dye pot !

It was from these dyes the Celt fashioned his gay tartans—it is from these dyes we still get our beautiful tweeds and tartans. Strange to say, the dyes, even shorn of their incantations and of their special hours of gathering, give results which are quite satisfactory.

So that September Andrew and Barbara fared forth on this High Adventure. It was a honeymoon trip, Andrew explained, which might last for years, however! He was sure that in New Zealand there were people competent to carry on the work, whereas for him and Barbara, Scotland, the land of the heather —land of the bens and glens—must ever be the homeland.

J. AND J. GRAY, PRINTERS, EDINBURGH